Malheur August

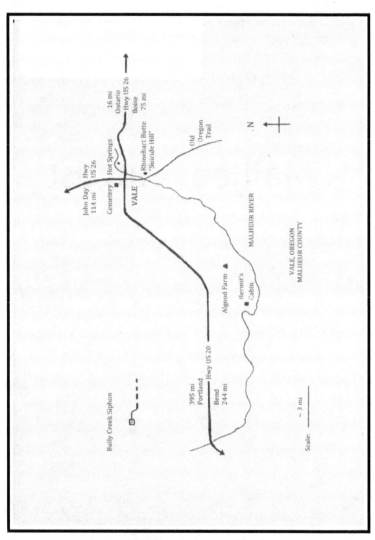

Map of Malheur River and Vale

Malheur August

by

Nancy Judd Minor

Golden Antelope Press
715 E. McPherson
Kirksville, Missouri 63501
2018

ISBN: 978-1-936135-61-5 (1-936135-61-2)

Library of Congress Control Number: 2018954384

Published by:
Golden Antelope Press
715 E. McPherson
Kirksville, Missouri 63501

Available at:
Golden Antelope Press
715 E. McPherson
Kirksville, Missouri, 63501
Phone: (660) 665-0273
http://www.goldenantelope.com
Email: ndelmoni@gmail.com

For Warden and Jerry

Acknowledgements

Many thanks to Elissa Minor Rust, the best daughter-editor a writer could ask for, and Jerry Kuykendall, who read drafts and gave endless encouragement. Thanks also to my family and friends who supported me and rejoiced in my accomplishment, particularly J. Minor, Quinn Minor, Beth Peterson Minor, Dennis Judd, Sandy Yates, and Nan Kammann Judd. Finally, I wish to thank all my former students through the years who taught me as much as I taught them and who inspired me to find my literary voice.

"It is those we live with and love and should know who elude us."
– Norman Maclean, *A River Runs Through It*

MALHEUR (French) = "mal" + "heur"
Pronounced = MAL hyure
Literally = "bad hour" or "bad time"
Probable translation = "misfortune"

The Malheur River winds its way through eastern Oregon on its journey to the Snake River. This river lends its name to Malheur County, the second-largest county in Oregon with a population density of only three people per square mile.

According to local legend the river received its name from French trappers who had stashed their pelts along its bank. When they returned to retrieve their cache the pelts were gone, probably taken by nearby natives. Because of that incident the unhappy trappers gave the river its name – "the Malheur," or "river of misfortune."

Vale (population 1817) is the county seat of Malheur County and sits in a narrow valley just two miles wide and fifteen miles long. With its welcome hot springs, Vale was an important stopping place on the Oregon Trail and wagon ruts can still be found just outside of town. The valley is surrounded by sagebrush-covered hills with the Malheur Butte, an extinct volcano, dominating the eastern end.

Chapter 1
The Algoods

(August 1971)

"It was the buzzards – that's how they knew he was dead," Betty assured Oleta after declaring that hearts would be trump.

From the couch across from the arched doorway separating the kitchen and living room, Jean stopped reading mid-sentence. *The hermit? Were they talking about the hermit?* She had been eavesdropping on Saturday night pinochle games between her parents and their neighbors, Betty and Leroy Fulmer, since she was a little girl, and even though she was now twenty-one and a senior in college, she lowered her well-worn copy of *Jane Eyre* and listened.

"Oh, good lord. Where'd you hear that – from the gossips at that church group of yours? You know it's not a quarter mile as the crow flies and I never seen no buzzards." Oleta laughed, a rollicking throaty laugh. "But I did hear the Oxmans smelled him – they live downwind, you know." Oleta winked at Betty and took a sip from her lipstick-stained highball glass. Betty snickered and Clete shot Oleta a withering look. Leroy, Betty's husband, kept his head down, eyes glued to his cards. Oleta ignored Clete and passed three cards across the table to Betty. "You're gonna like those cards, by the way."

1

Betty studied the cards and slid each one into her hand, collapsed them all into a stack and laid it face down on the table. She retrieved her cigarette from the ashtray and took a long slow draw, fanning herself with a cardboard Jesus fan. "You can laugh all you like, Oleta, but if you ask me, if the sheriff had done his job he would've moved him out of there a long time ago. I've been saying it for years. That man was a menace to decent society. Why, you couldn't even let the kids go fishing in that part of the river 'cause of him. I, for one, am glad he's dead." She ground out her stub in the ashtray and picked up her cards again, fanning them out.

Oleta leaned across the table toward Betty, her enormous breasts nearly spilling from her dress, "Well isn't that just real Christian of you? Did your church ladies tell you he was a black-sheep brother of one of the Navarro clan from up on the bench? That's what I heard. And you know those Basques are thicker than fleas on a stray dog and wilder than cowboys on the Fourth of July. A black-sheep Basque must've done something real bad." She leaned back and drained the last of her whiskey sour. "Hell, I'm sorry I never lit out across the field and made his acquaintance. I could've used some sizzle in my life." Oleta's bawdy laugh echoed in the cramped room. Jean winced.

"Oleta Algood!" Betty frowned, scrunching her thick brows into a single bushy furrow of disapproval. She laid down the queen of hearts, took the set, and played her last card. Tiny beads of sweat pooled on her brow and in the creases of her neck. She daubed her face with an elaborately embroidered handkerchief and fanned herself. A large moist patch had formed on her back and two more under each ample arm, the dampness spreading like a red tide. She shook out a new cigarette from her pack and tapped it twice on the table before lighting it. Leaning towards Oleta as though the dead man could hear her, she whispered from behind her fan, "What d'ya suppose he done?"

Clete slammed his cards on the table and aimed a wad of tobacco juice at the coffee can at his feet. His voice quivered with barely checked rage. "Are you two old hens gonna gossip or are you gonna play? Goddamn it, a man's pecked to death around here even when he's dead." He shoved his empty glass across the table. "Oleta, get me another drink."

Oleta shoved the glass back. "You can get your own damned drink. Hells bells, Clete. We was just talking. What the hell's the matter with you tonight?" Leroy gathered the cards and reshuffled, averting his eyes. Betty looked away and took another slow drag on her cigarette. The only sound was the whirr of the box fan and the chirping of crickets. A loose corner of the faded yellow wallpaper flapped with each rotation of the fan.

On the couch, Jean's stomach lurched. Over the years she had become fine-tuned to the nuances of her father's voice, the ominous lowering of pitch, the clipped cadence that signaled an impending explosion. Jean had been away the better part of three years, but five seconds of that voice and she felt the walls closing in. She burrowed deeper into the couch and willed herself to focus on her book.

Glancing up, she saw Clete's jaw quiver as he leveled an icy stare at Oleta. Oleta smirked, as though daring him to react, and fanned herself with a paperback novel. Clete stuffed another pinch of Copenhagen under his lip and lurched upright. As he shoved away from the table the heel of his hand caught the edge of the ashtray, upending it.

"Jesus H. Christ! What the hell was that doing there?" Before anyone else could react, Leroy righted the ashtray and began sweeping the butts into his hand.

"My fault, Clete. I think I might've pushed that over there a minute ago when I was dealing." Leroy's whispery voice and habitual slow delivery contrasted starkly with Clete's harsh, explosive outburst. Jean had a sudden memory of a game she and her cousin Will had played as children, in which they had assigned bird names to all the people they knew and the other person had to guess them. She couldn't recall what birds they had come up with for most people, but she did remember her father and Leroy Fulmer. Both she and Will had agreed that with his gentle demeanor and soft voice Mr. Fulmer was a Mourning Dove; her father was a Redtailed Hawk.

Leroy dumped the butts into the coffee can and sat back down. "Sorry about the mess on your floor, Oleta, but I think I got most of it." He pulled a handkerchief from his pocket and wiped his neck, then picked up his cards and spread them out in the same slow, methodical way.

Clete grunted and brought the bottle of Seagrams back to the table to fill his glass, ignoring Oleta's empty one. "Leroy, can I get you another drink? Oleta's sure as hell too damned lazy to lift a finger around here."

Leroy put his hand over his glass and shook his head, studying Clete anxiously. Clete spit into the coffee can at his feet and took another drink of whiskey, his spare body rippling tensely.

Before Oleta could respond, Betty reached over and rested her fingers on her arm. "Say, did you hear about Maxine Merkley? She up and left Ross high and dry. She's staying over to Ontario with her daughter. The word is she caught him fooling around with some other woman, don't know who. Can you imagine? Maxine Merkley of all people! I didn't think she had the gumption."

Oleta scowled at Clete. "Sounds like he was the one with the gumption. Or she was plain sick of him. Don't think I haven't given it a thought myself. And I wouldn't have no trouble finding another one neither, I'll tell you that."

Leroy cleared his throat and reached for the can of Copenhagen in his pocket. "You know, Clete, I was thinking that next weekend you and me might go up to the Owyhee Reservoir and do some fishing. We've both of us been working pretty hard the last couple of weeks." Leroy's voice was scarcely audible, but Clete visibly relaxed as he turned his attention to the fishing trip they began to plan for the following Sunday. Oleta rolled her eyes at Betty, but let it drop.

From her corner of the couch, Jean watched her mother from behind her book. Oleta was no beauty, but she had ample curves and an earthy sensuality that drew men. Watching her mother, Jean figured that she *wouldn't* find it hard to snare someone else. Jean couldn't remember a time when her parents weren't either fighting or on the edge of a fight. Why they had stayed together all these years was a mystery. As children, Jean and her sister Mae had dreaded Saturday nights when they would be awakened by the drunken sparring of their parents, the barbed insults piercing the papery walls of the tiny clapboard house. No pillow was thick enough to muffle the sound, no blanket warm enough to make them feel safe. They had only one another to cling to. Eventually the fight would end with Oleta threatening to leave, but the next day they'd get up and carry on as before, measuring off each miserable day together.

Jean wondered what it had been like for her older brother. Clark had left for teaching college when she was still in grade school and never came back to live with them. His visits home were regular but brief, and most of his time was spent with Oleta. Jean and Clark had never had a meaningful conversation. Perhaps it had been different for him. Perhaps there had been a time when Oleta and Clete had been happy, a time when Clark was younger, a time before she and Mae had been born. There were actually five Algood children, if she counted the twins who had died before Mae and Jean were born. Like Jean and Oleta, Clark had dark brown eyes and rod-straight hair. In the only two photos of the twins, those same chocolate eyes stare at the camera beneath mops of the same dull brown hair. Only Mae, the fine-boned blonde child with the pale aquamarine eyes, resembled Clete, which had always been a barb Clete used to goad Oleta. When he wanted to rile her, or when he was drunk enough, he'd accuse her of having affairs with one or the other of the neighbors, "because only one of those damned kids is mine."

Remembering those fights, Jean knew how much she wanted to avoid hearing one now, so she closed her book and slipped out of the room. Back in her cramped closet-sized bedroom she changed into her baby dolls and stretched out on the worn patchwork quilt that her grandmother had made for her shortly before she died. The faded window curtains hung slack and lifeless with not a whisper of breeze to disturb them. In the distance a lone coyote howled. Jean found the familiar sound comforting, companionable even. She picked a loose thread off the quilt and stared out the window at the clothesline silhouetted against the moonlit sky and the empty fields beyond. As she listened, the coyote howled again and was joined by another and then another in a howling cacophony. The odd discordant concert brought with it a turbid tumble of memory and she found herself missing Mae.

She and Mae had shared a small bed in this tiny room until Mae graduated from high school and left home. In the six years since Mae had walked across the stage and accepted her diploma she had returned only twice, even though Vale was only an eight-hour drive from Portland. But for some reason, a reason she could not explain even to herself, Jean came home every Christmas and at least once each summer. And every Christmas and every summer she wound up in this same room having the same interior conversation, wondering why she had come. Abruptly the coyotes ceased their calling. Jean waited, listened intently until they began again, then snuggled into the quilt to read, eventually drifting off to sleep.

* * * * *

"Jean, get your lazy college-girl ass out of bed and come help me with the milking!" The screen door slammed behind

Clete as he left for the barn. Jean, who couldn't even remember crawling between the sheets, clawed herself to wakefulness. Hanging over the sink in the kitchen, she splashed cool water on her face, willing the fog to lift. She felt leaden, hung over, even though the strongest thing she'd had to drink the night before had been a coke. *God, I could use some coffee*, she thought. The lowing cows told her Clete was moving the first group into the barn. Birdsong floated on the morning breeze; a garrulous rooster crowed repeatedly. Jean's barn clothes were where she had left them seven months before, still grimy, still sour with dried milk, still hanging stiffly from a hook in the kitchen closet. The overalls crunched as she stepped into each stiff leg. She struggled to pull up the jammed zipper, yelping when she nipped a finger. The milk-stiffened laces of her old barn shoes broke when she tried to tie them.

After checking to make sure Clete was inside the barn where he wouldn't see her, she sat down on the front step and blew on her pinched finger. Three half-grown yellow tabbies head-butted her, vying for attention. Martha, the ancient gray three-legged cat, purred and rubbed against her leg. Despite her sullen mood she stroked the cats, even smiling at the longhaired black cat perched atop the doghouse like a raven. When she knew she dared not wait any longer, she sighed and started for the barn, the yellow cats trailing behind her like a line of ducklings.

For the first half hour, as she filled the troughs with hay for the cattle, her mood was as sour as her clothes. Feeding the young calves, though, delighted her as it always did and she was smiling when she headed to the barn to help Clete with the milking.

The caustic stench of urine and manure permeated the barn, the pungent odor overwhelming her the moment she opened the door. The gorge rose in her throat. A half-gallon tin can sat on a shelf inside the door waiting to be filled with milk for the house; on the packed dirt outside the barn two large pans waited to be filled with milk for the cats. A skinny calico stretched out on the shelf next to the milk can and eyed her lazily. She squeezed past a complacent cow in the first stanchion and stepped over the shallow trough behind the stalls that caught urine and manure.

"I finished up with the calves. What needs to be done in here still?"

Clete was sitting on a stool behind the large Holstein at the far end of the barn, stripping the cow's udder of the milk the machine had left.

"Start on Patsy, she still needs to be stripped," Clete muttered from behind a massive flank.

Jean grabbed a stool and shoved her way between Patsy and another cow, pushing hard against Patsy to make room. She'd always liked this quiet part of milking, leaning her head against the velvety cows' flanks and daydreaming. The motor had been turned off and the barn was quiet save for the swishing of tails, the munching of hay, and the pssssst of milk hitting the metal buckets. Jean thought about the conversation she had overheard the night before.

"I heard you guys talking last night about that old hermit down by the river. Did you ever run into him?"

Clete grunted an affirmation.

"Did you know who he was?"

"Are you gonna grill me like your goddamned mother?"

Jean recoiled. Silently she finished stripping Patsy and moved her stool over to the next cow and buried her head in its flank. Molly shifted her weight, leaning into Jean and nearly knocking her off the stool. "Soo, Molly, soo," Jean cooed, stroking her side and shoving back with her shoulder.

Clete poured his full bucket into the milk can. "He wasn't nobody, Sis, just a crazy old coot. You think you can finish up here – or are you too educated for that now?" He mussed her hair and grinned at her, a crooked teasing grin.

"Sure, Dad." Jean warmed to the playful teasing she hungered for, but which came so seldom.

Clete patted the cow on the other side of Molly. "I'll come back and sterilize the equipment later."

As Jean finished stripping Molly, she heard her father outside talking to the cats. "Look what I got here for you – nice warm milk. Max, let me see that sore leg of yours. Now, don't fight me. That's a good fella." Clete had a soft spot for cats, always had. The place was overrun with cats. Many of the other farmers would drown extra litters of kittens to keep down the cat population, but Clete never did. Yesterday she'd seen him walking around the barn with a pair of kittens tucked inside his shirt, tiny whiskered heads peeking out of his collar. And it wasn't just cats. She'd see him out in the field talking to the cows, forehead to forehead, stroking their ears. Once he'd even tamed a mallard, which would waddle through the fields behind him like a dog. It nearly drove the real dog crazy.

Jean unlocked the stanchions and herded the cows into the pasture, then hosed out the barn, willing herself not to gag on the acrid fumes. The oppressive August heat was already building by the time she filled the tin can with milk and headed for the house, reeking of manure and sticky with sweat. Her mother had already left for her shift at the Starlite Café and the empty house was cool and still.

She had finished her shower and was toweling her dripping hair when the phone rang.

"Have you died of boredom yet?"

"Will!" Will, her crazy redheaded cousin, had been her pal and playmate her entire childhood. She hadn't seen him since Christmas. "Are you calling from Boise?"

"Nah. I love you, but you don't think I'd pay for long distance, do you? I'm at Mom's – had to come for her birthday yesterday and if I don't get out of here before they get back from Sunday School she'll strong-arm me into going to church this afternoon." Jean could almost hear Aunt Opal laying on the guilt trip.

"So what are you doing right now?" Will asked.

"I'm wrapped in a towel dripping water on the floor, actually."

"Well get dressed. I'll be there in twenty minutes."

Jean pulled her damp hair into a ponytail, brewed a pot of coffee, and sat on the porch to wait. Twenty minutes stretched into forty, then sixty, then ninety. By the time a roiling column of dust appeared in the distance, Jean had finished two cups of coffee and was hot, sticky, and annoyed. Will Lambson was her double-cousin, the son of Oleta's brother Harry and Clete's sister Opal, and Jean adored him. He had Howdy Doody hair and a screwball sense of fun, but the older she got the more his irresponsibility annoyed her. Will had more freckles than sense and couldn't work himself up to being serious about anything, except perhaps irritating his parents. Despite being double cousins who lived only eight miles apart in one of the most sparsely populated counties in Oregon, they were profoundly different. Jean, who had been raised on an isolated farm by parents who drank too much and fought too much, approached life with the same sober intensity she applied to her studies — even in play she held herself in check. Will, who had grown up in town in a strict Mormon household and had attended Church every Sunday for eighteen years, had turned into an undisciplined libertine. At Boise State he had shed the last remnants of sobriety. He had made it a point of faith to attend the first and last session of each of his classes and diligently failed every one of his final exams. When he failed completely at the end of the second term, his parents cut off his funds. In the four years since flunking out of college he had worked at the local Ford dealership, mostly hawking trucks to farmers. Asthma had kept him out of Vietnam. He and Darla, another lapsed Mormon from Burley, shared a cramped basement apartment with two other hippie friends.

Jean waited irritably at the gate as Will spun to a stop in a mustard yellow Mustang convertible. Will climbed over the seat and grabbed her in a tight hug then stood back and tugged lightly on her ponytail. "Nice touch. Makes you look old and sophisticated. Every time I see you, you look more and more like Liz Taylor. Except, of course, that you're skinny — and flat-chested ..."

Jean boxed him on the arm. "Enough already. You're not exactly Charles Atlas." Will was tall and rail thin. His hair had grown into an enormous red Afro that encircled his freckled face like the wig of a deranged clown. "That's some crazy looking hair. Cool tie-dye too. Did Darla make that shirt for you?"

"Hey. Darla's liberated, man. She doesn't make me anything. I bought it from a flower child on Haight-Ashbury last year. Cool trip, too. So where are Aunt Oleta and Uncle Clete?" Will tipped his wrist like someone drinking and raised his eyebrows.

"Not this early. Dad's out in the fields and Mom's at work. Can you believe I still have to help with the chores when I'm home? At least I don't have to hoe beets anymore. God, I hated that." She lifted her arm to his nose. "I probably still smell like a barn."

Will held her arm and sniffed it, then worked his way to her neck and her hair, sending her into another spasm of giggles. "Hm, an interesting bouquet. A hearty mixture of manure, sugar beets, and body odor."

Jean hit him again and pulled her arm away.

"Speaking of beets, guess who I ran into at the Stinker Gas Station in Boise? Alice McDermit. Isn't she that stuck-up cheerleader who sat on a lawn chair drinking lemonade while you and Mae hoed her beets that summer that Uncle Clete hired you out?"

"She's the one, all right. I can't believe he made us do that and I will never forgive her for rubbing our noses in it like that. The jerk."

"Well you will be happy to know that she must have gained

40 pounds and is frumpy as hell. She had two grubby kids in the backseat."

"It's karma. Serves her right."

"Hey, check it out." Will reached into his backseat and pulled out a six-pack of coke and another of Schlitz and held them aloft. "Guess which one's for me?"

Jean held open the screen door and Will put the beer and sodas in the fridge. He squeezed into a wobbly chair at the small Formica table, stretched out his legs with his hands behind his head, and looked around.

"This house has bad *feng shui*."

"It has bad what?"

"*Feng shui*. Darla's been studying it. It's something about how the house is laid out. The doors should be oriented so that all the good karma can pass through the house . . . or maybe so it stays in the house. I don't remember. But, whatever it is, this house ain't got it."

Jean looked around. "No, it sure doesn't. I just got home yesterday and they were at each other's throats by the time I went to bed. Oh, that reminds me. Remember that time when we were kids and we spied on that old hermit down by the river?"

"Oh, man. Are you kidding? I'll never forget that day. Joe William Hardy and Nancy Jean Drew solving *The Case of the Hermit by the River*. Hell, we must have hidden in the sagebrush behind that shack for two hours quivering in our boots and never even saw the guy. Remember that scorpion you almost stepped on? Scared the shit out of you."

"Well at least I missed it. Didn't you take two ticks home in your hair? Anyway, Mom and Mrs. Fulmer were talking about him last night. Somebody found him dead in his cabin a few weeks ago. I wonder who he was, don't you?"

"Whoa. I just had an idea. Let's go check his place out. You know, rummage around a little. Do some snooping, maybe see if we can discover some clues to who he was. We wouldn't even have to hide in the sagebrush."

"I don't know, what if ..."

"What if what? Come on, he's dead, man."

Jean hesitated. Going near the river made her anxious, maybe because as children they had been forbidden to go near the place. Perhaps that was part of the reason the adventure by the hermit's shack with Will had been such high drama so long ago. But the idea of reliving an episode of their childhood was irresistible.

"Ok. Sure. Why not? I'll throw together some sandwiches and we'll have a picnic by the river."

Chapter 2
Jean and Will:
The Hermit's Hut

Once the lunch was packed she rummaged through a box in the old stone room and found a battered straw hat for herself and a baseball cap for Will. Mashed by the hat, Will's hair billowed out at the sides and back. Jean could scarcely look at him without laughing.

They followed the same route they had taken ten years before, cutting through the Algood's east pasture and across the fallow fields and greasewood desert. It was already insufferable, even for August. In the distance superheated waves shimmered above white alkaline fields that glistened as though dusted with snow. At the edge of the Algood property, Will held the barbed wires apart while Jean climbed gingerly through, stepping over the remains of what looked like some kind of rodent. A lock of her ponytail snagged on a barbed knot, pulling her up sharply until Will helped her untangle it. As they neared the water, Jean wondered why the river had been off-limits when they were children. They had always played closer to the house, down by the drainage ditch or under the cottonwood grove, never here by the river. This stretch of the Malheur wasn't even much of a river this late in summer. Wide and shallow, it wasn't deep enough to swim in; better, rather, for wading and skimming rocks. Further downstream, however, were a few deeper pools where rainbow and bull trout spent their days sweeping their fins rhythmically in the current, a few growing to impressive sizes.

The hermit's shack was another quarter of a mile south, where the river made a sharp bend to the west before veering off again to the northeast. They caught a whiff of the outhouse before they saw the shack. A massive gnarly cottonwood hovered over it, one trunk-sized limb nearly resting on the roof. The riverbank was lush with willows and wild Russian olive trees, but away from the river there was little but greasewood and cheat grass. A lone jackrabbit surveyed them from a distance.

"Yow! Holy shit!" Will swatted madly at his legs. "Damned red ants!" He dropped the lunch sack and pulled off a sandal, hopping on one foot.

Jean helped him brush off the ants as he cursed and yelped then ran into the water. A welcome whisper of wind played with the tree branches and caressed her cheek. Beneath a cluster of willows, she burrowed a hole in the sandy riverbank to keep the bottles cool and hung the lunch sack from a low branch.

The crumbling sun-bleached shack was smaller and sadder than she remembered. A tattered piece of corrugated cardboard had been wedged into one of the windows in place of glass, a second window was encrusted with years of thick grime, and the weathered door dangled from rusty hinges. Scraggly, desperate weeds crowded the doorstep. Jean felt the whimsy of adventure evaporate like water in desert air. Something felt wrong here, out of kilter. Will seemed to sense her change in mood, for as she hesitantly pushed against the creaking door, he came up behind her and leaned in close to whisper in her ear.

"What if his ghost is hanging around? He might not take kindly to intruders. Wait. I think I hear moaning."

Jean rolled her eyes and pushed harder, shoving paper and debris out of the way as the door creaked open. The shack had only one room, not much larger than her parent's small living room. Decades of newspapers covered the floor to a depth of more than a foot in most places; against the walls magazines and catalogs were piled as high as the windowsill. In the center of the room a chipped green drop-leaf table tilted on an angle and a single chair lay on its side. A rusted metal bed frame with a sagging mattress leaned against the wall, partially covered by a WWII Army blanket and a bare striped pillow. Jean poked a pile of clothes with her foot – a pair of overalls, a ragged coat, one glove. A pot-bellied stove lurked in one corner. The inert air was suffused with the fetid, sour miasma of death and decay.

Will dug through the piles, shoving crumbling papers aside. Grinning broadly, he held up a yellowed Spiegel's cata-logue featuring women's brassieres. Ignoring him, Jean pulled a faded Life from mid-stack.

"Look at this. 1948. Twenty-three years ago. It's older than we are."

"Far out." Will sneezed violently three times in rapid suc-cession, sending dust flying, then wiped his nose on his upper sleeve.

"Geez, Wills. That's disgusting." Jean stepped around a particularly large stack of newspapers and rummaged through a pile beneath the window.

"What are we looking for, anyway?" Will kicked at a stack of magazines covered in mouse droppings. Reaching down he momentarily fingered a yellowed copy of *Look Magazine* and tossed it aside, sneezing again and again. "This place is killing me. Even Frank Hardy knew when to quit. I'll be down at the river when you've had enough – swimming in two feet of water."

After he left, the room felt even closer, stuffier, more claustrophobic. Jean stretched and shook her hands at her sides, an old habit she had when she felt anxious. Again she scanned the room, the table, the bed, the stove. Turning in a circle she surveyed it from all angles and finally realized what was wrong. There were no personal touches at all. No pictures adorned the walls, no family photos rested on a nightstand, no memorabilia collected dust. It was as if a cipher had lived here, someone with no family, no history, no personal life. The cabin held no clues at all, just emptiness. As she bent down to sift through another pile, Jean was filled with an almost incomprehensible grief.

"Pull it together, Jean," she told herself.

Cautiously, she picked up the corner of the blanket with two fingers to look beneath, checked under the mattress, peeked inside the stove. She was digging through one of the larger piles when she caught a whiff of something odd, something that at first she couldn't identify. Coffee, she realized. Ground coffee. She stood up and the smell dissipated. She turned around and scanned the cabin, but could not find the source. This place is giving me the creeps, she thought. Time to leave.

As she reached for the thermos of water she had set next to the door she smelled it again. Next to the thermos a rusted Folgers can lay on its side partially buried in papers. The top was covered with a scrap of yellowed newspaper held in place by twine. Jean turned the can in her hands and picked at the knot, but when it wouldn't give way, she tore the paper off. Curled inside the can, smelling faintly of coffee grounds, was a very old, very wrinkled photograph. Jean held the photograph by its crimped edges and stepped outside, blinking while her pupils adjusted to the light. In the picture four blonde teenagers leaned against an old black Ford and smiled at the camera. Jean perused the picture, holding it up close, then at arm's length. When she was sure of what she was seeing she took it to the water's edge and called Will.

"Wills, come here. I found something." Will was sprawled in the shallow stream soaking up the sun. He rose and shook off water like a puppy, then fished under the willows for a beer and a coke.

"Whatcha got?" he asked as he popped the caps and handed her the coke.

Jean gave him the photograph. "I found this in a coffee can in the house. Who does that look like to you?"

Will looked at the photograph. "Hot damn. That's Uncle Clete."

Clete was unmistakable. He was thirty or forty years younger, but it was definitely Clete. He was grinning at the camera, a hand-rolled cigarette dangling from his lip and a cowboy hat tilted rakishly on the back of his head. One of his arms was draped over the shoulder of the girl next to him.

Will examined the photograph like Jean had, tilting it first one way, then another.

Both Clete and the other boy in the photo were wearing Levis, but nothing else about them was similar. Clete had rolled up the sleeves of his white cotton shirt to show off his biceps. His dark blonde hair was parted on one side and combed back, a few locks straying over his forehead. The other boy in the photo, tall and rail-thin, smiled timidly at the camera, his nearly white hair cropped short and neat. He towered over the others and tilted toward them in his plaid farmer's shirt, holding his hat in one hand by the brim. The contrast between the two was striking.

The girls were sandwiched between the two boys. The girl next to Clete matched his height, even without the cowboy boots. She stared at the camera with a bold defiant smile, almost a smirk, and her eyes sparkled. She was not an attractive girl, but she was singularly interesting. Her jaw was somewhat too sharp for a girl, her figure too angular and bony, her nose a bit too large. She was dressed in dark trousers and a light blouse, a scarf tied around her neck. Her hair, bobbed to chin-length, was tucked behind her ears. She was nearly as thin as the tall gangly boy and stood arrow-straight, her shoulders thrown back. The second girl was exquisite. She was tiny and ethereal looking, her features carved like fine porcelain. She wore a flowered shirtwaist dress with a feminine lace collar and a softly flared skirt. Her long platinum hair was pulled up with a wide ribbon, and covered her shoulders in loose waves. She had one arm around the tall boy's waist and the other around the girl to her left.

"Damn, Jean, does your dad look cocky, or what? He's got sort of a James Dean thing going on there. That tall girl looks familiar too, but I can't put my finger on it."

"I can. I've seen a picture of her before at your house. That's our Aunt Cloris." Cloris was a mysterious figure in Jean's life. She was Clete's twin sister, but Jean had never met her. No one talked about her and it was understood that doing so was off limits. The little she did know about Cloris she had wormed out of Oleta.

"No kidding? Aunt Clara? She wasn't much to look at, was she?"

"Not Clara. Cloris."

Will took a swallow of his beer. "Clara, Cloris, whatever. That little blonde number is a knockout, though. The car's cool too – looks like a Model A."

Jean snatched the photo. "Who cares what kind of car it is? What I want to know is, what is a picture of my father doing in the old hermit's shack? That's the real question, isn't it?"

Later, after they returned to the house and Will had peeled out in a billowing cloud of dust, Jean opened her third coke of the day, a cold one from the fridge, and sauntered into the back yard. Leaning against the trunk of a craggy black locust tree, she stretched out her legs and rested the frosty bottle against her cheek. She savored the first icy swallow and paused for a moment to appreciate such a perfect thing on a blistering hot day. They had never had soda pop in the house when she was growing up, just Schlitz for Clete and Oleta. Perhaps stocking the fridge with cokes when she was home was her parents' way of killing the fatted calf. *Duly noted and appreciated*, she thought. She figured she had a good half hour before Oleta's shift at the cafe ended or Clete came in from the fields.

Shading the photo from the glare, she studied it. She was fascinated by how happy, young, and carefree they all looked. They must have been seventeen or eighteen, and the way they were standing, close together and touching one another, captured a genuine warmth and friendship. Jean considered her father. His grin was the cock-sure grin of a boy who knows he can charm any girl he wants. *No wonder mom fell for him*, Jean thought,*I probably would have too.* Jean was in high school when she did the math and figured out that Clark had been born barely five months after Clete and Oleta had married. In the photos in the family album, Clete's good looks were apparent, but never the full-throated joy of the young Clete in this photograph. The father she knew showed occasional flashes of that charm, but anger always lurked close beneath the surface.

Stroking Martha, who purred beside her, Jean studied Cloris. Jean had known about Cloris for years, but no one talked about her and Jean had no idea what had happened to drive a wedge between her and the family. Jean had always assumed that she was a prostitute or drug addict or something. In her more elaborate daydreams she had imagined Cloris as an exotically beautiful international spy. Jean had seen a grainy photograph of her in an album at Will's house, but she was considerably younger than the girl in this picture. But studying her now, it was clear that Cloris was neither exotic nor beautiful. The same chiseled features that had made Clete strikingly handsome had made his twin sister almost homely.

From the photograph, however, it seemed that even without Clete's looks and charm, her personality was as dominant as Clete's. She didn't look to Jean like the prostitute type, nor could she imagine someone that self-assured as a derelict on skid row.

Jean's reverie was broken by the sound of Shep barking in the distance. *Dad must be coming in from the fields.* She swigged the last drop of coke, stretched like a cat, and headed into the house to start supper. *Maybe tomorrow I'll go see Cass*, she thought.

* * * * *

The next day Jean finished her morning chores and drove into town, slowing as she approached the Chevron Station and the city limits. It was nearly noon when she pulled up in front of the Vale Mercantile. The door to the store had not yet closed behind her when she was grabbed by Cass and nearly smothered by two enormous breasts.

"Jean! When did you get home? Oh, Honey Child, let me give you another hug. I could squeeze you to death."

"It's good to see you too, Cass." Cass Simpson was her mother's oldest friend and the only adult in town that even children called by her first name. All the other adults were referred to as Mr. or Mrs. or Aunt or Uncle, but Cass was always just Cass. She was a giant of a woman, more than six feet tall and about a hundred pounds the other side of plump. The dress she wore, a dark green polyester embellished with large yellow roses, accentuated her girth. As long as Jean had known her Cass had been heavy, but she seemed to grow exponentially larger with each passing year. Her gravelly smoker's voice boomed, accompanied by a rollicking good-natured laugh.

Jean disengaged herself and smiled at Cass's tightly permed and hennaed hair. "If you aren't too busy, do you think you can get away to have lunch with me?"

"You bet I can. Honey, this is Monday. No one's been in here for an hour."

Cass strode into the back room and came out with an oversized yellow handbag, the same color as the roses on her dress. "Hey, Peggy. I'm leaving to take Jean here to lunch."

At the Dairy Queen across the street they settled into a red vinyl booth. Johnny Cash's deep bass boomed from the jukebox. After they placed their orders, Jean pushed the photograph, still trailing the scent of coffee, across the table to Cass.

"Will and I found this yesterday in the hermit's cabin by the river. You know the one, don't you, out on the Malheur beyond the east pasture? We heard that the guy died so we were sort of snooping around and I found this in a coffee can."

Jean watched Cass's face as she picked up the curled photograph. Her brow furled, her manicured red nails clicked nervously on the Formica tabletop. She pursed her brightly painted lips and opened her mouth to speak, then abruptly closed it again.

"Hey, Cass, Jean." Jean and Cass both looked up into the eyes of Robbie Hawk, the younger brother of one of Jean's classmates, who set their burgers, fries, and drinks on the table. Cass's demeanor altered instantly.

"Hey yourself! I hear you've been spending a lot of time with Linda George. You better be treating her right or you'll have to answer to me, ya hear?" Cass winked at Jean and Robbie flushed a bright crimson, smiling sheepishly. When he headed back to the counter, Cass tore into her hamburger, setting the photo off to the side where she could still see it out of the corner of her eye. She bathed each French fry in a sea of ketchup and mayonnaise before popping it in her mouth.

Jean picked at her food and finished her coke, waiting until she became impatient. "So, who are they? And why would a picture of my Dad be in that old hermit's shack?"

Cass licked her fingers and wiped sauce from the corner

of her mouth. "I can't imagine what it would be doing there. Kind of odd, isn't it?" Cass finished off the last of her burger.

Jean had not been prepared for Cass to be evasive and felt herself getting annoyed. "Cass, I know that's Dad's sister. Do you know what happened to her? No one will talk about it. And who was that old hermit anyway?"

Instead of answering, Cass called Robbie back and ordered a banana split and two spoons, bantering with him as though stalling for time. When Robbie left she turned back to Jean.

"I figured we don't get to see each other every day, so we might as well splurge a little." She cleared her throat. "I'm sorry, Jeanie. I can't really help you much. I really have no idea what happened to Cloris. She left after high school and then the war was on. I think I heard once that she and Clete had some sort of falling out."

"Well, didn't Mom ever talk to you about it?"

"No, can't say as she did. Cloris was three years ahead of us in school so we didn't know her all that well."

"But what about these other two? Who are they?"

Cass fidgeted. "I can't rightly remember their names; they were from out by Willow Creek or Brogan I think. A brother and sister. Like I said, they were all older than we were and you know how that is when you're in high school." She handed the photo back to Jean. "Ah, here's our banana split. How long are you here for?"

Cass steered the conversation toward Jean and her life at school. Jean barely touched the ice cream, but Cass wolfed it down and looked at her watch. She pulled out a mirror and reapplied her lipstick. "I've got to get back so Peggy can take her lunch."

The photo hovered on the table like a wall between them. Jean pointed at it, a trace of irritation in her voice. "Wait, Cass. Do you know who that hermit was or what this picture was doing in his shack?"

Cass gave her a quick hug. "Hard to say, never heard a

word about him. We'll talk later. Got to run."

Chapter 3
Cass and Oleta: 1937

Cass's heart pounded as she rushed, as much as a person her size could rush, across the steaming pavement away from Jean and the torrent of memory that threatened to swamp her. She tore through the front door, cheeks flushed and head lowered, gave Peggy the briefest of nods, and bolted into the restroom.

The moment the door was closed her knees buckled and she sunk heavily onto the floor, sobbing as the past pulled her into its eddy, taking her back through the years to a time when she was only fourteen....

(August, 1937)

Summers were always hot in eastern Oregon, but the summer of 1937 was scorching. Each day melted into the next as the thermometer teetered between 100 and 110. Corn stalks, normally tall and green, stood shoulder high, the ears small and deformed; grasses and weeds turned from brown to sere. When the fair opened that third week of August, everyone in the county was desperate for anything that would take their minds off the merciless, endless days that blistered into sweaty

sleepless nights. For a week dark clouds had gathered each afternoon and hovered, glowering, but no rain fell. The oppressive supercharged air pressed down, relentless. The winter
before had been no less punishing. A long string of sub-zero
days had taken many of the cattle, and now, with the drought,
fear and anxiety stalked the valley. Conversations at the feed
store or at the Five and Dime touched on little else.

The Malheur County fair was the highlight of every summer for Cass and her best friend, Oleta Lambson. Most of the
kids were stuck on farms working six days a week with only
the occasional Saturday to see their friends, but once the fair
came they had four glorious days to be together. Oleta and
Cass had saved their babysitting money for months and had
arranged for Oleta to stay with Cass in town. Cass lived on the
western edge of town with her parents and older brother Joe
in one of the few Victorian houses in Vale. The yellow house
with white trim had been ordered by Cass's grandfather from
Sears and Roebuck in 1908 and delivered via railcar. With
three bedrooms and an indoor bathroom, it was more than
twice the size of the home that Oleta shared with her parents
and four brothers. Whenever she could, Oleta stayed in town
with Cass, not only so she wouldn't be marooned ten miles
from town with no friends, but also so she could have a bath
without heating water and pouring it into a metal tub. With
four brothers she didn't have to help that much with the barn
chores; but feeding and cleaning up after five men, as well as
running a household and tending a garden, was almost more
than one woman could handle, and her mother did not like to
let her go. Cass and Oleta had plotted far in advance, getting
permission during the dark winter months when the workload
was lighter. By the time August arrived Oleta's mother reluctantly let her go.

That first day of the fair was lovely. The oppressive heat
had given way, at least momentarily. Only cottony wisps of
cloud broke the expanse of robin's egg blue that stretched to

the horizon. The loamy tang of freshly cut alfalfa lingered in the air, wafting from nearby fields and mixing with the tantalizing aroma of freshly popped corn. Oleta and Cass had spent hours getting ready. Oleta's grandmother had helped her work over one of her mother's old dresses to give it a more stylish look. She'd sewn pads in the shoulders to mimic the styles worn by the big Hollywood stars Oleta loved, and had fitted the bodice tightly around her well-developed bosom. As soon as they were out of sight of her parents, Oleta undid the top button.

"Oleta! People are going to talk about you."

But Oleta just laughed and aped Mae West, "It's better to be looked over, than overlooked." Since they had gone to see *Belle of the Nineties*, Mae West had become Oleta's obsession. She liked her deep husky voice and the way she swaggered and leered at the men. She liked that she wasn't little and slender like Claudette Colbert, but full-figured and loud like Oleta. She liked her sassiness. She had even tried to fix her hair like Mae's, in tight finger waves with pin curl bangs, but her rod-straight hair wouldn't hold the curls.

Oleta adjusted her dress and attempted to fluff her hair. "I just wish I could do something with my hair. As soon as I'm old enough I'm going to get a perm and bleach it like Mae West does."

"You know your mom won't let you do that."

"She can't stop me, not once I'm eighteen." She examined herself in a piece of mirror she had pulled from her purse. "How am I ever going to get the boys to look at me with hair like this?"

Before Cass could respond, Oleta spotted a group of teenagers entering the midway. "Oh look, there's Sandy Condon and her cute brother!"

Oleta shouted Sandy's name and waved her arms until Sandy saw them and the group made their way through the crowd to join them. Sandy was with two cousins from Nampa

whom Cass and Oleta had met before, and the five girls immediately started an animated conversation. Oleta tried flirting
with Sandy's older brother, but he was clearly disinterested
and left abruptly after a few minutes. The chattering freshmen
girls moseyed up and down the midway, laughing boisterously
and looking at the booths. At some point Cass and Oleta broke
away and ambled off by themselves, ending up in front of
Madame LaFarge's Eye of Knowledge booth. Oleta was keen
on having her fortune read, but was loathe to hand over ten
cents of what little money she had. Cass volunteered to do
the job for half, but told her she would have to die young.
The two friends dissolved into a spasm of giggles, annoying
the barker who was trying to drum up customers. Eventually
they each got a two-cent cone of cotton candy and meandered
over to the barns to look for the boys. When the girls were not
wandering the midway, they spent their time in the animal
barns. Most of the boys had one kind of animal or another to
show, and where the boys were, they wanted to be.

Oleta's brother Harry was showing a yearling Guernsey he
had named Mrs. Murphy, and Cass's brother Joe had entered
three lop-eared rabbits he had raised in their back yard. Cass
and Oleta finished their cotton candy amidst a warren of rabbit
cages containing rabbits of all sizes and breeds, from exquisite
longhaired Angoras to diminutive Dwarf Rex. Cass adored her
brother Joe, even though he was often impatient with her,
especially when Oleta was around.

"God Almighty! What's the matter with you? I just brushed
them for the judging and you've got your sticky fingers all over
them." Joe snatched a rabbit from Cass and returned it to the
cage with the others. Oleta rolled her eyes at Cass, but Cass
felt terrible.

"I'm so sorry, Joe. I didn't think. Can we do something to
help? Brush him or clean the cage or something?" Her voice
quivered on the edge of tears.

"Well don't cry about it. Just go somewhere else." Cass noticed, to her embarrassment, that Joe glanced at Oleta's tight dress before turning his back on them. She suggested to Oleta that they go over to the cattle barn to see Harry's heifer.

Oleta hooked her arm through Cass's and leaned in. "Did you see the way Joe looked at me?"

"He did not. Gross. That would be like Harry eyeing me." Cass scanned the crowd thronging the midway. "I wonder if Archie's here?" Cass had developed a crush on Archie Simpson right before school ended and talked about little else much of the time.

"Maybe. And maybe he'll have a cute friend with him." Oleta and Cass giggled and strolled arm in arm into the cool shade of the cattle barn. Oleta had little interest in cows, or anything else having to do with the farm. Her future, she was certain, was far from Vale in a world populated by sophisticated people living in tall buildings with elevators and lap dogs. Cass, however, liked the cows with their long curved eyelashes and soft flanks. She even thought the pigs were cute, especially the huge sows with gigantic litters. As a town girl from a small family she led an easy existence, free of the onerous chores that made up the daily routine for Oleta and most of her other friends.

Mrs. Murphy, Harry's Guernsey heifer, was located in a stall near the center of the barn. It was evident that the stall had been recently cleaned; even the straw had been swept into a tidy pile. Harry, however, was nowhere to be found. Oleta plopped down on a bale of straw while Cass stroked Mrs. Murphy's neck. A tinkle of bell-like laughter floated over from the stall immediately across the aisle from where they were waiting with Harry's heifer.

Oleta grabbed Cass's arm and whispered, "Oh look, it's Clete Algood and his friend. Isn't he dreamy?"

Clete had his forehead butted up against a big-eyed Jersey's forehead while he stroked her ears and crooned "Daisy, Daisy, give me your answer, do/ I'm half-crazy all for the love of you." Annie Mueller was sitting on a nearby straw bale, giggling. Cass thought she had the most exquisite laugh she had ever heard. Annie was a wisp of a girl, barely five feet tall, with a slight frame. Her pale aquamarine eyes sparkled as she watched Clete. Her brother Karl, more than a foot taller than his sister and scarecrow thin, was brushing the heifer. A hint of a smile pulled at his mouth as he listened to Clete sing. Clete's sister Cloris perched on the top rail of the pen chewing on a piece of straw.

"Hey, Clete, is that how you get all the girls to fall for you?" Cloris teased. "Why don't you try that song on Annie and see how it works – and don't forget to rub her ears."

Cass and Oleta choked back their laughter so the older kids wouldn't know they were listening in. Cass thought Clete was handsome, but she was not enamored with him and certainly not with the painfully shy Karl Mueller. Both the senior girls, though, mesmerized her – Annie due to her beauty and Cloris because she was so radically different from any of the other girls in school. Cloris was the only girl they knew who always wore pants instead of dresses, except at school where she had no choice. All the other girls were dressed in their finest for the fair. Annie dazzled in an Alice blue dress with match-ing ribbon, but Cloris wore a pair of pleated brown trousers cinched high on her waist. She had probably made them her-self, but they actually looked good on her with her lanky body and long legs. Many of the girls had been tomboys when they were kids, but Cloris was seventeen and still a tomboy.

When Cloris joked about Clete singing to Annie, Annie flushed a deep crimson. Clete looked over at her and ran his fingers through his hair to push it out of his eyes.

"No," he said, "I do believe Annie deserves a prettier song, something special just for her. I'll have to think on it."

Annie smiled and blushed. But something palpable had passed between them. Cloris looked at her, then at Clete, and her face said she didn't like what she saw. A shadow passed over Karl's face as he gathered some hay to feed his heifer.

"Did you see that?" Oleta hissed. Before Cass could respond Harry returned and struck up a conversation with Clete. Cass and Oleta stayed until they got bored then went in search of Archie and any other friends they could find.

The next three days flew by, as the heady days at the fair inevitably did. Saturday night was Oleta's final night in town and the last time the girls would be together until Oleta's family came back to town for supplies, which would probably not be for several weeks. The theater was showing the same comedy the girls had seen the night before, but movies only cost a dime and Oleta always wanted to go to the movies, regardless of the film or how many times they had seen it.

The Rex Theater was packed on Saturdays; the younger kids filled the seats for the matinee and teenagers came at night. All the girls watched the stars to learn how to wear their hair and what kinds of clothes to copy, even what to say. Oleta was so star-struck that she vowed to name all her children after movie stars. Oleta and Cass had a running argument going over who was dreamier, Clark Gable or Gary Cooper. Oleta hadn't stopped talking about Clark Gable since seeing him in *Mutiny on the Bounty* the summer before. The pre-movie newsreel had shown him with Carole Lombard on his arm, dripping glamour like she dripped furs. In those days Oleta nattered incessantly about finding a way off the farm and ending up in Hollywood.

Cass and Oleta were among the first to arrive so they could claim the two seats tucked in next to the projector room at the top of a short staircase in the balcony. A loose metal grill on the floor between the two seats allowed them to hear any conversations taking place below in the lobby. Even more important, from their elevated perch they could see anyone who sat in the seats down below as well as watch the couples who came up to sit in the balcony. The newsreel had already begun when Clete and Annie came in, holding hands. Annie was looking at Clete like he was Clark Gable himself. Oleta elbowed Cass and pointed them out. Clete and Annie sat in the furthest, darkest corner of the theater. Through that entire movie the girls spent as much time craning their necks to watch Annie and Clete as they did watching Gary Cooper and Jean Arthur, transfixed in a way that neither could explain.

Chapter 4
An Accident

The cloying scent of Taboo lingered in the air after Cass left. Jean dawdled in the red vinyl booth, scraping the last bits of chocolate from the dish and licking them off her spoon. Out of sorts, she tucked the wrinkled photograph into her bag and opened the door into a wall of super-heated desert air. August in the high desert was so arid that the slightest gust would lift clouds of loosened topsoil, swirling them into fleeting dust devils that bounced and zigzagged across the fields, carrying with them the pungent scent of onions from the acres that had been planted south and east of town. The smells riding on the wind conjured up some of her best memories – hayrides, days at the fair, corn feeds at the Legion Hall with freshly-picked corn boiling in huge galvanized tubs, fresh tomatoes and ripe melons. Her irritation floated away on the desert wind by the time she had driven the few blocks to the courthouse.

As a child, endless Saturday hours had been whiled away in the tiny library squeezed into one room above the courthouse. Saturdays were town days for the family and magical in the summer. Her mother would give them each fifty cents and set them loose. She and Mae had had a set routine – a visit to the drug store for penny candy, sunflower seeds, and comic books followed by a movie or a visit to the swimming pool and ending with a stop at the library for a week's worth of books. They always had time to kill, so they would browse the shelves to see if anything new had been exchanged with another library in the county. Later, they would wait in the car, often for hours, reading books and eating sunflower seeds, until their parents stumbled out of the Golden Slipper to take them home.

Virgie Condon had been the librarian as long as Jean could remember. Jean spotted her from the rear, standing on a ladder re-shelving books from a cart. Jean didn't know how old Virgie was, but Jean had dated her grandson in high school. Virgie was a short stout woman with bowl-cut grey hair and strangely thin ankles. Over the years Jean had always been fascinated by her physiology – how could someone as solid as Virgie have the ankles of a fifteen-year-old? It defied nature. Jean wondered how those tiny bones supported that kind of mass. Virgie turned her head when she heard the door open.

"Hello, Mrs. Condon. Any new books today?"

"Well Jeannie! Aren't you a sight for sore eyes? Will you be home for a while?" Virgie and Jean talked about books and Virgie's grandson. As always, Virgie gave Jean a list of book suggestions and sent her out the door with a stack to see her through her visit. The drive home gave her time to think. She had come to town expecting Cass to give her all the answers and instead had come away even more confused by Cass's behavior. By the time she pulled into the driveway she had made up her mind to bring up the photograph with her mother as soon as an opportunity presented itself. What did she have to lose?

Shep did not come to greet her as he normally did, but she could hear him in the distance barking, probably at a gopher, his nemesis. Jean inched around the cats sprawled on the front steps and carefully opened the screen door so she wouldn't knock one off. After dropping the library books on the bed she tuned the radio to a Boise station that played mostly popular rock and folk music, and stuck her head in the fridge to figure out what to make for supper. A package of ground beef was un-thawing in the fridge, dripping blood onto a lower shelf. Jean tossed the meat in a bowl and grabbed a white porcelain basin on her way out to the garden to pick the vegetables. Shep was still barking when the basin was full and she returned to the house. She had a meatloaf in the oven and was singing along to "Raindrops Keep Falling on My Head" when her mother entered, rear first, pushing open the screen and swinging around to deposit two grocery bags on the table.

"It's hotter 'n a bitch in heat out there," boomed Oleta. "Thank God you're here to fix supper. I just don't have it in me. My feet are killing me and the tips were lousy today. Damned cheapskates."

Oleta lowered herself heavily into a chair and pulled off her shoes. Beads of sweat had gathered in the creases of her neck and stains were growing beneath the sleeves of her pink uniform. She hiked her skirt up and peeled off her damp nylons, stuffing them in her pocket.

Jean snapped off the end of a large ear of corn and tossed it in the sink. "I saw Cass today. She hugged me so hard she nearly knocked the breath out of me."

Oleta smiled wearily. "Well, you know she loves you kids like you was her own. We ought to have her out for supper one night while you're home, but your dad's been so damned ornery lately – and he doesn't much like her on a good day. Maybe you and me and her can have a girl's night out, maybe go over to the Eastside Café in Ontario for some of their good shrimp. I got Friday off."

She leaned back in the chair and grimaced. "Jeannie, could you hand me a cold beer?" She rubbed her temples. "My head is killing me today. And do you mind turning that radio down? I can't do anything about that damned dog."

Jean reached over and switched off the radio. "Shep's been barking nonstop ever since I got home. Dad must be out in the north forty if he can ignore that. Maybe I ought to go check."

"If you do, take a hoe in case he's after a rattler or something."

Jean smiled inwardly. She had never once seen a rattler anywhere near the house. "Mom, no snake would be out on a day like today – it'd sizzle like a steak!"

Oleta closed her eyes and held her head in one hand. The harsh afternoon light deepened the shadows under her eyes, aging her.

"You look exhausted, Mom. Why don't you take some aspirin and go lie down until supper? I can handle everything here."

The door banged behind her as she stepped into the blinding sunlight. Old grey Martha stretched out on the front step in the shade of the eves and swished her tail in a lethargic greeting but did not lift her head. Between the house and barn the parched earth was blanketed in a desiccated layer of cake-flour fine dust. Jean picked up a stick and trailed it in the dust behind her as she walked. She loved the feel of the warm powder billowing up between her toes; as a child she had delighted in making dust angels in the barnyard on hot August days. She followed the dirt road out of the barnyard past the abandoned outhouse, around the chicken coop, and into the western pasture, following Shep's frenzied barking. The deeply rutted lane was lined with ripe milkweed bursting their pods and cheerful sunflowers. Jean hummed as she walked up a short rise leading to a narrow plank bridge that crossed over the drainage ditch fifteen feet below. The water in the steep ditch was so low this time of year that it disappeared completely beneath a tangle of watercress.

As Jean neared the bridge she spotted Shep at the same instant she saw the tractor, laying on its side in the bottom of the ditch. Clete lay motionless, his face pressed into the hillside and his upper torso twisted grotesquely against the steep slope, his legs disappearing beneath the two-ton John Deere. Jean threw the stick and ran.

* * * * *

"When did she say she was leaving?" her mother asked again as she continued her agitated pacing, wearing a path in front of the double grey doors leading to the Intensive Care Unit. Clark, Jean, and Oleta had been in and out of Clete's room all day, when they were allowed in, but most of the time they had maintained their vigil in the sterile pea-green waiting room. Clark had left Spokane within an hour of Jean's phone call Monday evening and had driven all night. Now he dozed in one of the chairs, legs stretched out and head thrown back, snoring softly.

Jean took her mother's arm, coaxing her toward a chair. "Mom, remember, I told you already. Mae couldn't leave right away. She's got to take care of some things at work first, but you know she'll come as soon as she can." Oleta collapsed into the chair and began sobbing again. Jean rested on the chair arm and stroked her mother's hair, willing Cass to come striding down that long empty hall.

Cass had stayed with them all night, only leaving in the morning after Jean's aunts and uncles arrived. She had promised to return later when everyone left to take care of their barn chores, or sooner if they needed her. Jean struggled with the urge to call her, fought against the fatigue that ate into her shoulders and back. If Jean had had her way, Cass would never have left. Without Cass the very ground beneath her felt less solid, as though she were sinking ever deeper into a bottomless morass. Aunt Opal, on the other hand, had spent the day reading her scriptures and babbling incessantly, bubbling over with nervous energy and repeatedly referring to her brother Clete in the past tense. By the time Opal had left in the middle of the afternoon–the last of the extended family to do so–Jean's nerves were stretched to the snapping point.

Her arms and legs hung like heavy weights, attached to her body, but somehow foreign to her. When she spoke she heard a stranger's voice, tinny, strained, and muffled. Everything, in fact, felt detached from her, like watching some other Jean acting out a part in a surreal drama. Her mind kept returning to the horror of those first minutes, tossing them around, thinking of alternatives, "what if's." What if she had checked on Shep when she first got home. What if she had never gone to town. What if. When she had gotten to Clete he was still breathing, but barely. Had it been earlier in the summer he would have drowned; instead the impact with the hardened mud had snapped his neck. Her first impulse had been to try to move the tractor, but realizing that was impossible, she had done the only thing she could do, run back to the house for help, yelling all the way. Her mother met her as she rounded the corner past the barn and stayed with Clete while Jean called for help. With trembling hands, she had dialed the operator, and listened to her disembodied voice explain the situation, clearly and almost calmly. She had been told to stay right there and an ambulance would be dispatched. Her next call was to Leroy Fulmer. In his quiet, calm voice he had told her he was handing the phone to Betty and he wanted her to explain everything to her so she could get help while he drove over. Before she was off the phone, Leroy and his son were already driving out toward the drainage ditch.

More neighbors soon arrived, followed by Betty Fulmer. For the first time in her life, Jean was grateful for bossy, take-charge Betty Fulmer. Betty assigned a neighbor woman to wait for the ambulance and sent Jean to help her mother. By the time Jean got back at the accident site the men had managed to leverage the tractor off Clete's legs, and Leroy, who had been a medic in World War II, was immobilizing his neck. The additional half hour waiting for the ambulance had seemed endless, each minute an eternity, as she listened to Clete's labored breathing, to Oleta's hysterical crying, to Shep's agitated whining, to her own erratic heartbeat.

When Jean started to climb in the ambulance after the attendants loaded Clete for the ride to the hospital in Ontario, Betty had taken her car keys so that she and Leroy could deliver the car to her. She had also assured her that the cows would be milked and all the animals fed and cared for as long as the need existed. The last thing Jean remembered before the ambulance doors closed was seeing Steve Fulmer and Roger Oxman herding the cows into the barn. By the time Betty and Leroy delivered the keys to the hospital, Betty had arranged meal deliveries for them for the next week, with more to be planned later, and had set up a complex schedule for caring for the farm that involved nearly a dozen families. When Betty handed her the schedule and told her she would be reminding everyone daily, Jean had started to cry for the first time. Betty had reached over, put her hands on Jean's shoulders, and looked her in the eyes.

"Jeannie, listen to me. It won't do to have you fall apart right now. You've got to buck up, be tough for your mom. She's not strong, you know, so you've got to be. Take a few deep breaths. You're tougher than you think you are."

Betty's words found their mark, and to her surprise, Jean realized that she was, in fact, tougher than she had thought she was. She had wiped her eyes, shaken her hands to calm her nerves, and gone back into the room dry-eyed.

The prognosis was not good. Clete had stopped breathing shortly after his arrival at the hospital and had been placed on a ventilator. They had waited with Clete's sister Opal and her husband Harry, Oleta's older brother, and, of course, Cass. When the young doctor had walked out to talk to them, Oleta had looked at his eyes and the sympathetic narrowing of his brows, and collapsed before he even spoke. He introduced himself as Dr. Rayburn, and he was brutally frank. Clete's injuries were devastating. He had broken his neck beneath the fifth cervical vertebrae and Dr. Rayburn suspected severe spinal cord injury and probably brain damage. If he did survive, which was unlikely, he would never walk again. In addition, his pelvis and both legs had been crushed and he appeared to have at least some internal bleeding. Clete was in a coma and Dr. Rayburn told them to prepare for the worst, that Clete was unlikely to survive the night. In the hours since then there had been little change. He had survived the night, but he had not improved.

When Clark began to stir Jean felt a flood of relief. He yawned and rubbed his eyes and without a word sat down on the other arm of Oleta's chair and put his arms around her. Oleta leaned into his chest like a small child. "Jean," he said, "you look exhausted. Why don't you go get some coffee or something?"

"I'm alright."

Clark's bloodshot eyes bored into hers. "You are not alright. As your older brother I'm ordering you to take a break. Now!"

"I guess I could call Mae again to find out when she's coming. She should be off work by now."

"Good idea. And get something to eat while you're at it."

Chapter 5
The Algoods Gather

Jean found a payphone at the end of the hall near the tiny cafeteria and placed a collect call to Portland. After she filled Mae in on their father's condition the phone went silent.

"Mae? Are you still there?"

"I'm sorry, Jean. Sorry you are having to deal with this. How's Mom doing?"

"She's a mess, can't stop crying, won't stop pacing. Cass was here all night, but she left this morning. Hopefully she'll be back soon. Clark got here about 5:00 this morning and Mom won't let him out of her sight. When can you leave?" she asked, her voice shaking.

There was another long pause. "We're awfully busy at work right now. I can't just pick up and leave. I could try to get Friday off and come for the weekend maybe."

"Friday? Maybe? Mae, he could be dead by the weekend. Mom needs you now!"

"Jean, Mom doesn't need me. She wants me. Those are two quite different things. She's got you and Clark and Cass and probably everybody else in town. Dammit, Jean. That place is toxic to me. I stopped caring about him a long time ago. You'd be better off if you did too."

Mae's bitterness stunned Jean into speechlessness. And then she started sobbing, wrenching, gasping, out-of-control convulsions. She slumped to the floor with the telephone receiver clutched to her chest, struggling to get a breath.

"Jean, Jean," she heard Mae calling to her, the sound muffled. "Jean, I'm so sorry. Jean, answer me."

Jean lifted the receiver to her ear and choked out a whispery, "Sorry."

"Oh, Jean, don't. Don't be sorry. I'm the one who should be sorry. God, I'm a meaner bastard than he is. Oh, shit. I shouldn't have said that either. God, I'm so sorry. Forget everything I said. I'll come as soon as I can. I'll work things out today and leave first thing in the morning or Thursday at the latest. OK?"

Jean sobbed out a "K" in reply.

"Are you sure you're all right, Jean?"

Jean managed a raspy reply. "It's been a really, really hard day. Come soon."

"Be tough. You know what mom always told us — buck up. Lean on Cass and Clark until I get there. Can you do that?"

After more reassurance from Mae, Jean placed the receiver back in the cradle and rested her head on the phone to regain her composure. She could feel more tears lurking beneath the surface waiting to erupt. Sighing, she went into the women's bathroom to wash her face, staring at her reflection in the mirror. Bloodshot rhuemy eyes stared vacantly back at her.

"You look like hell, Jean," she told herself. Before going back upstairs she stopped at the hospital cafeteria for a cup of black coffee and a stale donut, then sat at a table by herself staring into space. When she felt she could trust her emotions again, she fished two Excedrin out of her purse, swallowed them, and headed back upstairs.

* * * * *

Jean was startled by the sound of voices and fought to wake

up, swimming through the viscous fog, clawing her way to consciousness. When she sat up the hammering in her head nearly knocked her down again. A dull ache stretched down her back snaking its way into her left hip. She rubbed her cramped neck, surprised that she had fallen asleep. Buttery streaks of late afternoon light spread from floor to ceiling on the inner wall. She looked around. On the opposite side of the room from their family a wizened old man with a large hooked nose held his head in his hands, the golden rays encircling his hoary hair like a halo. Next to him a large middle-aged man sporting the same nose and an enormous belly flipped through a *National Geographic Magazine.*

Dr. Rayburn, the young doctor attending to Clete, had just grabbed a chair and was pulling it over to Oleta. Each one of her forty-eight years was etched onto Oleta's face. Her normally well-coiffed hair lay plastered flat against her head revealing iron-grey roots. Without her girdle, and slumped as she was, she seemed more frumpy than voluptuous. All of her mother's charm stemmed from her brassy, loud personality, her bright red lips and revealing dresses, her bawdy sense of humor. The total package worked like a costume an actress might don to play a part. Now, sagging against Clark, she reminded Jean of the jackrabbits that Shep sometimes hunted down – cornered and defenseless.

"He's stabilized for now, that's the good news," Dr. Rayburn began, "but I don't want to give you false hope." The doctor went on to explain that he still did not think Mr. Algood could pull through although he had plateaued for the time being. He could not breathe on his own and was unresponsive, both very bad signs. Nevertheless, Dr. Rayburn felt that the family needed to go home and get some rest. "This could go on for some time."

Oleta reacted as though she had been slapped. "What kind of person are you? You don't up and leave someone to die alone. That's not what family does, at least not this family! I want to see my husband right now! Why can't we stay back there with him? What the hell kind of place are you running here?" Once again she collapsed into hysterical weeping and Jean was mortified.

Clark seemed to know precisely what to do. Clark, nine years her senior, had always been just another adult in her life. By the time she was in fifth grade, he had already left home for Oregon College of Education in Monmouth, the first one in the extended family to go to college. Oleta adored him, but he and Clete could hardly be in the same room together. Clete had never forgiven him for going to college instead of staying to work the farm, like Leroy's sons. Clete had often complained that Clark was "too damned stupid to do anything useful."

Jean wondered what Clete would think of Clark's usefulness now. Jean could take care of the details; she could get help, work with Betty to make arrangements, make the phone calls. But what Jean could not do was calm her mother. From the moment Clark had arrived he had taken over and, like Cass, seemed to know instinctively what she needed. It was Clark's shoulder Oleta leaned against, not Jean's. It was Clark she asked to clarify the doctor's words, not Jean. Clark could jolly her into eating, get her to stretch out on the couch and nap, and now he got her to go home. He did not try to use logic, as Jean would have. Instead he told her he agreed with her absolutely, one of them had to be there at all times in case Clete got worse. He intended to send Jean home with her, but Jean knew Oleta would need Clark to settle her down enough to go to sleep. Besides, after the nap she'd had, Jean was getting her second wind. Reluctantly, Clark agreed to leave, but said he would set the alarm for 2:00 a. m. to come back to relieve her.

After Clark took their mother home, Jean was left by herself in the sterile waiting room; even the old man and his rotund son were gone. After fifteen minutes alone in the room, the cold green walls began to close in on her. She looked over at the battleship grey doors behind which her father lay hooked up to a machine, a machine that was the only thing keeping him alive, and walked over to the nurse's station and asked to be allowed in to see him, alone.

He lay on the bed, a large tube snaking down his throat. An ominous panel monitored his heart rate and blood pressure, the air reverberating with a steady beep, beep, beep. Between his right temple and ear a vivid purple bruise was spreading and his face was more swollen and less recognizable than earlier in the day. Jean took his limp hand and squeezed. Nothing.

She cleared her throat and leaned in close. "Dad, it's Jean. Mom and Clark went home, but I'm still here. One of us will always be nearby if you need us." She squeezed his hand again. Again, nothing.

She tried to think of what else she should say, what words he would want to hear if he could hear her, but the silence in her mind was drowned out by the steady metronome of his heartbeat. She studied his face and allowed herself to consider what she had been stuffing into her subconscious for twenty-eight long hours: that she had no idea what she felt about her father dying, or even what she was supposed to feel. Her father was lying in a hospital bed hovering between life and death, but she was not overwhelmed by grief or love or any of the other emotions she thought she should feel. Instead she was almost brought to her knees by a shattering sadness, a sadness that welled from some deep hidden place where it had been lurking for years. And even though she had never experienced real grief, she knew this was something else entirely. If he died tomorrow, she realized, she would not feel grief then either. And this realization was the saddest thing of all.

When the doors closed behind her ten minutes later, she was greeted by a cheerful booming voice pumping oxygen into the stagnant waiting room air.

"Jean, sugar, you look like you've been through hell and back out the other side." Cass was wearing a crisply ironed lavender print dress. Her hair had been freshly hennaed and styled, her long acrylic nails painted a crimson red.

"Oh, Cass. You have no idea," she said giving her a grateful hug. "You look amazing though. Did you get your hair done?"

"Damned right! You didn't think a little thing like this would be enough to make me cancel my cut and color, did you?" Cass enclosed Jean in her fleshy arms and snuggled her against her chest. Jean could barely stretch her arms around Cass, but she clung to her like a barnacle on a ship.

"I brought you something." Cass peeled herself loose and reached for two A & W bags. "I even talked them into selling me two mugs, but the frosted part we'll have to do without." Cass set two slightly smashed hamburgers, both oozing sauce, on the coffee table along with two large bags of fries, two mugs, and a quart of root beer.

Jean's stomach lurched. "That's really sweet of you, Cass, but there is no way I could eat a thing. Even looking at that makes me nauseous."

"You can drink, though, right? I'll tell you what. You humor me and force down one of those french fries while I pour you a root beer."

Reluctantly, Jean agreed to try. After one tentative nibble on a french fry she stuffed the entire thing in her mouth and picked up another and another, then she grabbed a hamburger. She attacked the lukewarm burger with the ravenous gusto of a starving person, licking every dab of sauce off her fingers when she finished. After drinking the root beer, she belched so loudly that it echoed in the empty room. They both started to giggle, then snort, then howl, doubling over in hysterical tear-filled laughter. When the laughter abated, Jean kicked the sandals off her feet and pulled her legs up, trying in vain to wipe a large sauce stain from the front of her wrinkled t-shirt. She gave up and tossed the napkin in the bag. Slipping her arm through Cass's arm, she leaned her head on her shoulder. After a minute, she turned her body so she could look Cass in the eye. "Cass, I need to ask you something."

"Sure, Hon, fire away."

"Cass, you've been my mother's closest friend her whole life, and I need help understanding her right now. She can't love my dad. I mean, how could she? She's talked about leaving him for years. They can hardly be in the same room without snapping at each other and I've heard them call each other names I wouldn't even repeat. So, what's with her now? She acts as though the world is dropping out from under her feet, as if she can't live without him. I don't get it. Is it an act, or what?" Jean surprised herself by the acid that dripped from her question. *I sound like Mae*, she thought.

Cass leaned back in the chair wearily and reached over to squeeze Jean's hand. "Oh, honey. That's not easy to explain. It's complicated. She's complicated. *Marriage* is complicated, and this one more than most. They started out kind of rough and they've been through a lot together, you know, what with the twins and all. And sometimes the wrong two people get tangled up together and can't ever seem to unwind themselves."

"But I still don't get . . ."

Their conversation was interrupted by the clicking sound of someone in heels walking briskly with short mincing steps. A moment later Aunt Opal rounded the corner. Opal's hair had been teased into a huge bouffant flip cemented firmly into place, the ends turned up like points on a meringue. Her short pudgy frame was draped in a brilliant orange dress covered in gigantic white and yellow blossoms. She looks like the wallpaper at a Motel 6, Jean thought. The clicking had come from a pair of matching orange pumps. On her arm dangled a small white handbag fastened with an ornate daisy-shaped clasp; in the other hand she clutched a brown paper sack.

"Jeannie, you poor, poor dear! I'm sorry it took me so long to get here. I had to stop at the church first — Tuesdays are Relief Society nights you know – and give a lesson to the sisters. I probably should have asked someone else to do it, but to tell the truth, it helped take my mind off your dad for a while."

Opal leaned over the couch to kiss Jean, then plopped down next to her and pulled off her shoes, rubbing her insteps. "All the sisters said to tell your mom how concerned they are and that they're praying for the family. They're all real worried about her. Everyone was asking how they could help, so I told them I would add them to the schedule for meals and farm chores and what not. I'll go ahead and call Betty Fulmer. You shouldn't have to worry about a thing for a long time."

Opal reached over and covered Jean's hand with both of hers and looked her full in the face. "Now, I know your folks and I don't always see eye to eye on things, but do you think your mom would mind if your Uncle Harry and one of the other elders gave your dad a priesthood blessing? I know it would put my mind at ease. Would it be alright if I go ahead and set that up too?"

Jean groaned inwardly. Opal had converted to Mormonism before she married Harry Lambson and had never given up on converting her brother, who made no secret of his disdain for the church— or for her, for that matter—but none of this had deterred her. Jean was grateful for the help and knew most of the members herself, had even gone to dances at the church as a teenager with some of her Mormon friends, but she didn't appreciate Opal foisting her beliefs on them, not right now. And she knew her father would not like it at all if he were aware of it.

She glanced at Cass, who just grinned. "Thank you, Aunt Opal. I appreciate you calling Betty and you be sure to tell everyone at the church how much we appreciate everything they're doing for us. I think, though, that you need to talk to mom about the prayer, don't you?" Jean knew that Opal would never bring it up with Oleta. She and Oleta had clashed more than once over religion and Clete and Oleta's lifestyle.

Opal pursed her lips and took a deep breath, patting Jean's hand before removing hers. "Well all right then, I'll do that. I know Harry will be disappointed, though, if he can't at least do this one last thing for Clete."

Opal smoothed her skirt, then reached for the paper bag she had set on the couch and handed it to Jean. "I've got a little something for you that Will had me pick up."

Jean looked inside the bag and chortled with delight. She glanced over at her Aunt Opal, who was grinning. Opal winked. "What, me worry? Nothing like comfort food, eh?" The bag held the latest edition of *MAD Magazine*, a pound of black licorice, and a dozen of her favorite Idaho Spud bars.

Opal slipped on her shoes and hoisted herself to a standing position. "Jeannie, would you go in with me to see your dad? I don't think I can face being in there alone right now."

Jean sighed, handed Cass the bag, and leadenly followed Opal back through the bleak gray doors.

Chapter 6
Cass and Oleta: 1940

Alone in the waiting room Cass turned an Idaho Spud bar over in her hands and peeled back the brown wrapper. Her thoughts returned to Jean's question about Oleta. *How much should I tell her*, she wondered?

(February 1940)

By the time she and Oleta turned sixteen, Cass had heard Oleta catalogue the flaws she saw in herself so many times that she could recite them in her sleep. Oleta hated the gap between her front teeth. She hated her coarse, dull brown hair. She hated that she was big-boned and full-bodied. She hated her big nose. She hated that she had to wear glasses. When Oleta looked in the mirror she didn't see any of her good qualities; instead she saw a magnified version of every tiny imperfection, real or imagined, and believed every cruel thing she'd ever heard from five teasing brothers. To Oleta it wasn't enough to be attractive; she had to be movie star beautiful–and she wasn't. But what she lacked in beauty she made up for in brass, the brassier the better. It was almost as though she thought that if she acted like Mae West, maybe she'd turn into Mae West. Even Cass tired of her constant

flirting. By their junior year in high school she and Archie
Simpson were going steady and his disapproval of Oleta had
caused a crack to form in the two girls' relationship. Cass
found herself wincing when Oleta's boisterous laugh echoed
down the hallway, and started finding excuses to spend less
time with her. When she was with Oleta for any length of
time Archie's silent censure ate at her.

In February of that year someone at school cooked up the
idea of having a wiener roast at the mouth of the huge irriga-
tion siphon up above Bully Creek. The siphon was eight feet
in diameter and ran dry in winter. It was one of those ideas
that started out small and snowballed to include even the kids
who had already graduated but still lived in town. All the popular kids were planning to go and Oleta wasn't about to miss
it. Cass wanted no part of it. She'd hated that siphon ever
since she's seen a friend's dog sucked into it two summers before; but Oleta could be a force as strong as any siphon, and
Cass was pulled along with her. Archie was sick, which made
things easier for Cass, so she and Oleta rode up with Cass's
brother Joe.

By the time Joe pulled his dusty red Ford off the highway and onto the rutted track leading to the siphon, the last
light was fading, taking with it the only warmth of a cloudless
February day. The truck bounced and groaned, high center-
ing momentarily on a gnarly patch of greasewood. After crest-
ing a low rise, Joe made a jolting U-turn and stopped several
feet from a dented Model A. Loud laughter and a cacophony
of voices echoed from the bottom of the ravine. Joe rushed
ahead, leaving the girls to find their own way. Oleta and Cass
climbed gingerly over protruding roots and around bushes,
following the dim trail in the sparse moonlight, their breath
encircling them in cloudy billows. As they crested the hill a
reedy male voice called up to them.

"Oleta! Cass! We was wondering if you was ever going to
get here."

Oleta looked at Cass and rolled her eyes. "Why is it always Melvin who's watching out for me? What a creep."

Melvin was part of a small group feeding a large bonfire in the dry canal bottom thirty feet or so from a smaller fire just outside the mouth of the siphon. When they saw the girls they waved and shouted to them. Melvin raced uphill to meet Oleta and Cass, the earflaps on his hat fluttering as he climbed, and stretched his hand out to Oleta to steady her. Oleta ignored the hand and hollered to a couple of her friends, brushing past Melvin as though he were a phantom. Cass took the disappointed hand and thanked him profusely, embarrassed over Oleta's rudeness. With Melvin's help she made her way down the treacherous embankment. Oleta's raucous laugh already rang out louder than any of the others. Several dozen teenagers huddled around the fires, laughing and chatting with friends. Overhead the cloudy arm of the Milky Way sparkled with millions of stars, undiminished by the small sliver of February moon.

A rollicking laugh caught their attention and they saw Clete standing in the mouth of the siphon wearing a weathered cowboy hat with an incongruous periwinkle blue scarf wrapped around his neck. He jumped up onto a large boulder, waving his arms and calling for everyone to gather around. Cloris joined him and they began singing, he in a high clear tenor, she in a deep contralto.

> *Come on and hear, come on and hear Alexander's Ragtime Band*
> *Come on and hear, come on and hear 'bout the best band in the land*
> *They can play a bugle call like you never heard before*
> *So natural that you wanna go to war*
> *That's just the bestest band what am, oh Honey Lamb.*

"Come on, everybody sing." Clete led the singing, which was tenuous at first, but soon increased in enthusiasm and volume with Cloris and Clete's harmonious voices rising above the others.

Around the crackling fires, everyone seemed to be caught up in the spell Clete was weaving. When the sing-a-long petered out, Clete dropped down on one knee in front of Annie, took her hand and began to sing *Heart and Soul*. When he crooned the lines,*"Oh but your lips were thrilling, much too thrilling/ Never before were mine so strangely willing,"* he pulled Annie to her feet and kissed her, knocking his hat off in the process. In the flickering light of the bonfire, it was impossible to see her blush.

The spell was broken when Willard and Melvin held aloft a bundle of sticks and called out, "come and get your wieners." Oleta huddled around the larger fire flirting with a boy from the football team while Cass squeezed around the smaller fire to find a spot behind Joe. It was warmer inside the mouth of the enormous pipe, although the black void echoing hollowly behind her was unnerving. She fought the impulse to push her way back outside, just so she could watch Annie Mueller unnoticed. Like most people she knew, boys and girls alike, Cass was fascinated by her. Annie and Cloris had been working in Boise since graduating nearly two years before and Cass had not seen her for nearly that long.

Annie had always seemed otherworldly to Cass, with her golden hair and pale blue eyes. The only time Cass ever saw her in trousers was that night. Several of the more daring girls were starting to wear them, but not Annie. Annie's slender neck was wrapped in a periwinkle scarf that matched the one Clete wore, and tucked in next to Cloris she appeared as tiny and delicate as a wood nymph. Clete bent over and whispered something in her ear and she laughed, a tinkling laugh like an exquisite crystal bell.

As Cass sat there watching them, sometimes talking with Joe and the others, Oleta leaned her head into the pipe holding aloft two skewered hot dogs and shouted, "Cass, come get your dog!" Her braying laugh reverberated against the metal and echoed in the blackness.

Everyone turned and looked in her direction, which was probably what she wanted, Cass thought, and Cass reluctantly got up and made her way around the crowd and out into the gap between the fires.

"So, what's going on with those two?" Oleta pointed with her hot dog toward Annie and Clete.

Cass smiled. "Beats me. But I heard a rumor that they're planning to get married in a year or so. He sure acts like he's crazy about her. Isn't she marvelous?"

"Marvelous? Oh, swell, you too? What's so marvelous about her? She's got no personality, none. And, hell, she ain't nothing but a scrawny little stick. He'd never marry her. From what I hear he likes girls with some curves to them, girls like me. I bet you I could break it up without hardly trying."

Cass was stunned. "Oleta, I can't believe you said that. Why would you want to do that? What's she ever done to you?"

"I don't have to like her just because all the rest of you think she's some kind of precious porcelain doll. And if I can take him away from her, then he can't be all that crazy about her anyway. You can think any damn thing you want. I'm going to go sit down by him right now."

And she did. She squeezed into the space between Clete and Joe, shoving Joe aside, and started chattering away. Oleta had her moments, but this was the first time Cass had ever seen her be scheming or hateful. A wave of sadness washed over her. Cass felt so depressed that it was all she could do not to cry, let alone pretend she was having a good time. She was cold, miserable, and more than anything else she just wanted to go home. She found a spot behind all the others in the siphon where she wouldn't have to talk to anyone. A slight breeze blowing into the siphon forced her to keep shifting to stay out of the path of the smoke. When she wasn't dodging smoke she was plastered against the cold lifeless metal, fighting the stinging in her eyes and the creeping numbness in her feet.

The black void behind her echoed ominously. It was while she was turning her back to the fire to avoid the smoke that she saw Annie's brother Karl hiding in the shadows deeper in the siphon, at the edge of the light and far from the heat.

Since leaving high school Karl had become ever more shy and reclusive. He never went to parties or dances. That he was here now must have been due to Annie and Clete. While they were in high school Annie had watched out for him, as though he were a younger brother, not an older one. Their mother was dead and their father had sold out and moved away the summer after Annie finished school, so all they had left was each other . . .and Clete and Cloris. There had been some talk in town about him, talk that he was acting strangely after Annie and Cloris moved to Boise. Joe even said something about seeing him at Dentinger's Feed & Seed, pacing in the back of the store muttering to himself. Some folks said that he had gotten so peculiar that no one would hire him unless Clete worked with him. The word was that he wouldn't talk to anyone but Clete, not even in the bunkhouses. Thus Cass was startled to see him standing in the shadows, leaning against the harsh metal as though trying to dissolve into it.

Someone started another song, a round, but it petered out quickly. Outside the siphon the frigid night was taking a toll and people were beginning to leave. Annie stood up, rested her hand lightly on Clete's shoulder for a minute, then worked her way back to Karl. Cass watched as Karl leaned over to hear her whisper something to him. She pulled on his arm, urging him toward the fire but he shook his head vehemently and shrunk back even further. She nodded, took his arm with both hands and rested her head against his shoulder, settling into the back with him.

The moment Annie left Clete, Oleta pounced. Cass heard

her boisterous laugh rise above the other voices. Shifting posi-
tions, Oleta grabbed Clete's arm momentarily for balance before telling a loud suggestive joke, provoking more laughter.
To Cass the hollow yawning void behind her was less ominous
than the performance playing out in front of her. Clete, however, did not take the bait. He stood up, tossed his stick on
the dying fire and said, "Hey, where's my girl?" As Cass went
around the dying embers one way, grateful beyond measure
to leave that siphon, Clete went around the other side to join
Annie and Karl in the murky shadows at the back.

After that wiener roast in February, Cass stopped seeing
Oleta entirely. Oleta's reputation went from bad to worse and
she started dating Willard, one of the wildest boys in their
class. Several times Oleta tried to patch things up, but Cass
rebuffed her.

In early June Cass ran into her at the Merc. Oleta was
alone, flipping through a rack of light summer dresses near the
back of the store. Cass knew that Oleta had never had a store-
bought dress in her life, but she always liked to look at them,
something they used to do together. Sometimes they would
both try them on, just to get ideas to copy. Cass's first thought
was to leave, but Oleta looked so incredibly sad, as though she
were wrapped in a shroud of melancholy, that Cass's resolve
gave way.

"Is something wrong, Oleta?"

Oleta started at the sound of Cass's voice, then began rear-
ranging her face and body the way a person might rearrange
the furniture in a house. Her shoulders lifted, her chin jutted
out, her mouth reformed into the semblance of a smile.

"No. I'm fine. I was planning an outfit, that's all. You
startled me. How's Archie?" She spoke to Cass as if to a casual
acquaintance, but she avoided Cass's eyes, instead studying a
lace collar on a dress. Her hand trembled slightly.

Cass felt every second tick off, one after another, as they
talked around each other, neither of them able or willing to

cross the chasm that had opened between them. After what seemed an eternity, Cass extricated herself and left. She didn't see Oleta again until the Fourth of July.

* * * * *

(July, 1940)

In New York City each year began with the drop of the ball in Times Square on the first of January. In the high sage-brush desert of far eastern Oregon, it began with the Fourth of July. In Vale, the four days leading up to the Independence Day celebrations were the focal point of the year. Cowboys competing in the rodeo circuit arrived from states as far away as Oklahoma and Texas to compete for purses in the Vale Rodeo. Bronc-riders, calf-ropers, bull-riders. Clad in leather chaps and well-seasoned boots, rodeo cowboys and cowboys off the ranches suddenly appeared around town, especially at the half dozen saloons that had sprung back to life in 1933. For four days the town acquired a rougher texture as a wild-west spirit suffused the valley of church-going farmers. Every night was a party, beginning with a rodeo and ending in the wee hours with a bottle of bourbon. Two big events were the high points of the celebration – the suicide race and the final July 4th rodeo.

In the late afternoon on the third day of the rodeo the competing riders would make their way up Rhinehart Butte, which looms 500 feet above the rodeo grounds on the eastern edge of town. When all the riders were in place, a blast of dynamite would signal the start of the race. Horses and riders would hurtle down the steep incline, plunge into the shallow river, then race for the rodeo grounds on the opposite shore to claim their prize and signal the start of the rodeo. Local boys joined with rodeo cowboys to prove who was the most daring as the horses struggled to retain their footing on the loose sediment.

Of all the riders in the rodeo, the winner of the suicide race was the most reckless.

An uneasy relationship existed between the townsfolk and the cowboys. Everyone loved the exhilaration of the rodeo, the breathless bravado. For four short days men and women alike shed the daily drudgery of responsibility. For four short days they lived on the borders of a fantasy west, the anything-goes wild west of Jim Bridger and Wild Bill. In reality, though, the farmers of the valley were descendants of a more domestic sort – the plodding pioneers who had braved the mountains and deserts in wagons filled with children and dreams of a homestead. Their grandparents and great-grandparents had come to put down roots, to stay put. But being responsible, while laudable, is hardly exciting – especially not to young women and men on the cusp of adulthood. All the parents in town knew the appeal of the seemingly carefree life that cowboys lived. They felt it themselves. And they also knew that along with their saddles the cowboys that rode into town every July carried with them more than a little whiff of danger.

For every year since they had been in the fifth grade, Oleta Lambson had stayed in town with Cass and her family on the Fourth of July. In the years that Oleta's family could, they brought her into town. In other years Cass's father had driven the twenty miles round-trip to fetch her, then another twenty to return her home. This year, though, Cass felt none of the thrill of the approach of July, only the oppressive, relentless heat. On the last week in June she was stretched out in a swing on her broad front porch listlessly reading *Gone with the Wind* for the second time. Scarlett had just tricked the hapless Frank Kennedy into marrying her when another Frank, the mailman, Frank Hunsaker, called to Cass.

"You're looking mighty comfortable. Best way I can think of to spend a day."

Cass rolled out of the hammock and walked over to the picket fence, hand out-stretched for the mail. "Thanks, Mr.

Hunsaker. You're early today."

Frank pulled a large handkerchief from his pocket and wiped his forehead. "Trying to beat the heat. It's a scorcher. There's a letter in there for you, too. You take care now."

Cass instantly recognized Oleta's rounded childlike letters and ripped open the envelope.

> *Dear Cass,*
>
> *I haven't been able to stop thinking about you since I saw you at the Merc three weeks ago. You asked me if I was ok and I said I was but I lied. I'm not ok at all I'm miserable. We've been best friends forever and I miss you. I would do anything to fix things. Harry has got to go to Nyssa on Monday. He could drop me off and we could spend the day or maybe even longer? Please write me. I'm really really sorry and I will try to be a better friend.*
>
> *XOXO,*
>
> *Oleta*

Cass read the letter over and over again while perched on the edge of the hammock. Archie was gone all summer working on his grandfather's farm in Idaho and she was lonely. And she missed her friendship with Oleta. Dreadfully. She went inside and scribbled a hasty reply, telling Oleta to come and stay until the fifth, like she always did; telling her that her dad would take Oleta home, like he always did; that she was still her best friend, like she always would be. She addressed the letter and was out the door speed-walking to the post office within fifteen minutes.

* * * * *

Oleta and Cass started talking from the moment Harry pulled up in front of Cass's house and Oleta opened the car door. Cass's mother made a big fuss over her, hugging and kissing her and showering her with the affection Oleta never experienced at home. She had even made a chocolate chiffon cake, Oleta's favorite dessert. The girls talked through supper, through washing the dishes, through a slow walk to the Dairy Queen and back. They talked into the wee hours of the night until fatigue caught up to them and they finally fell asleep. They tripped over their words, stumbled over each other's sentences, giggled and laughed and talked some more. By the time they were drawn downstairs the next morning by the smell of sizzling bacon and hot biscuits, it felt as though they had never been apart. Later that day they were in the stands with the rest of the crowd when the suicide racers thundered into the arena.

"Look at him. Isn't he the cat's meow?" Oleta said, as the winner of the suicide race was introduced. He was a wiry dark-haired cowboy, tanned and cocky.

He had torn through the gate on a mottled Appaloosa, its wild mane flying. He circled the ring and dismounted with a flourish, holding his hat by the brim and waving it at the roaring crowd. Oleta yelled and whistled so loudly that he pointed his hat at her and winked.

After the rodeo they headed over to the carnival, riding the Ferris wheel twice and filling up on ice cream sodas. Eventually the two split away from the rest of the crowd and strolled down to the bridge. They watched the nighthawks swooping and diving after insects in the fading light, shrieking when one zipped past their heads making a sharp squeak. They delighted in the welcome evening breeze, the full moon when it rose, and the pleasure of being together. Again the two girls talked late into the night, even though Cass had a nagging headache.

By the time they awoke on the morning of the fourth, Cass was running a high fever and her throat was so sore she could scarcely swallow. Her parents debated whether they should

find another place for Oleta to stay, but decided that Oleta
had already been thoroughly exposed to whatever Cass had.
They didn't want Oleta to miss all the fun, so they insisted
that she go to the rodeo and the dance with the other kids
from school and Joe would take her home the next day.

Cass drifted in and out of sleep that night. Even a swallow of water was agonizing. Once she woke up and wondered
where Oleta was before sinking back into a fevered sleep. She
awoke again as the sky began to lighten and saw Oleta curled
up on the edge of the bed, still in her dress. Cass asked for water and Oleta brought her a drink, helping her to sit up. The
next morning Cass was scorching to the touch and muttering
about large spiders on the wall. Cass's mother rang the doctor, then Cass's father, urging him to come home. Sometime
around noon a tense and silent Joe drove Oleta home.

Several days later Oleta got a short note from Cass's mother
telling her that Cass was dangerously ill with scarlet fever. For
weeks Cass slid in and out of lucidity as the fever raged. After
the excruciating rawness of her throat finally abated along
with the fever, she began to improve, but then the fever returned. This time the fever brought with it painful swollen
joints and a lethargy so extreme she could scarcely lift her
head. Cass spent the rest of the summer recovering from
rheumatic fever, missing not only the Fourth of July, but also
the county fair and the first two weeks of her senior year.
Oleta wrote frequently, but until the middle of August Cass
was too weak to even respond. Cass always wondered how
things would have been different, how many lives would have
taken different paths had she not become ill that summer of
1940.

When Oleta walked into Cass's bedroom the last week of
August, the late summer air was already pregnant with the
essence of early autumn. The earthy smell of freshly cut alfalfa
mixed with the refreshing hint of sage. Nearly two months of
forced inactivity had given way to a restless ennui that was a

marked contrast to Cass's normal exuberance. Oleta had been allowed to visit once, several weeks before, but only for half an hour. In order to force Cass to rest, her mother had restricted not only visits, but also excitement of any kind. By the time Oleta arrived for an afternoon visit the last week of August, Cass was champing at the bit to leave her house.

"Tell me everything that's happened this summer. I want all the gossip. Every single juicy bit. Don't leave out a single thing."

Within minutes, Oleta had Cass chortling over the romantic intrigues and foibles of her classmates, particularly Melvin Porter's pursuit of Sarah Bennett, one of the cheerleaders, beginning at the rodeo dance and continuing at the fair. She howled over the image of Melvin cutting in when Sarah was dancing with one of the cowboys from out of town, and his cluelessness when Sarah kept dodging him by ducking in and out of the animal barns at the fair.

"So what about you? Are you still dating Willard or have you moved on to someone else now?"

Oleta bit her lower lip and her eyes twinkled. "Honestly Cass, I don't even know where to begin. I want to tell you everything, but you've got to promise me that you won't be mad."

"Why would I be mad? The only thing that will make me mad is if you don't spill everything — now. Tell me!"

Oleta twirled a lock of hair and chewed on her thumbnail for a second. "Do you remember that cute cowboy, Burl, who won the suicide race?"

Chapter 7
Oleta and Cass:
Secrets

(August 1940)

Oleta considered skipping the rodeo dance, but decided that since Cass needed to rest anyway she might as well go for a dance or two, just to see who was there. She stopped at the bathroom before entering the dance hall and studied herself in the mirror. Hair – starting to wilt in the heat, but the wave was still holding. Cute new dress with red buttons. Nice body. Not too bad, she thought, except for the crooked teeth and stupid glasses. I've got to remember not to smile too big. She applied a fresh coat of crimson lipstick and unbuttoned her top button, plumping up her breasts and adjusting each one to show to more advantage, then tugged on her skirt and adjusted her belt. Not bad, not bad at all.

Oleta had barely entered the room when she spotted Sarah Bennett dancing with the darling cowboy who had won the suicide race. Figures, she thought. No glasses, wavy blonde hair, button nose. No figure though. And she was just in time to watch when brainy Melvin Porter tapped Burl on the shoulder, cutting into their dance. She expected Burl to knock Melvin halfway to Boise and from the look on Sarah's face that would have been fine with her. Instead, he bowed deeply to Sarah and handed her over to Melvin saying, "It looks like you got yourself an admirer here. She's all yours, Bud."

Burl scanned the girls lining the hall and, spotting Oleta, headed straight for her.

When he stopped in front of her he doffed his hat. "Howdy there. I was hoping you might be here. Been watchin' for ya."

Oleta felt like she'd fallen through a rabbit hole like Alice in Wonderland. Burl whirled her around the floor for the first couple of dances, and then pulled her in tight for a slow dance. Oleta was so giddy she thought she might actually swoon, like Carole Lombard in *My Man Godfrey*. Blissfully she pressed herself against him and followed his lead. When the heat in the dancehall and crush of bodies became too oppressive they went outside for some air.

He rolled a cigarette and offered one to her, but she shook her head. "Say, how would ya like to meet my horse, Samson?" he asked.

"Are you kidding me? I'd love to!"

Burl ensnared her waist with his arm and they walked slowly toward the stables. As soon as they were in the shadows, he leaned down and kissed her neck, then pulled her in close for a long, wet kiss. She was surprised at how small he was. Standing together in the shadows kissing she realized he was not any taller than she was, even wearing cowboy boots, and probably weighed less.

At the stables, while they both stroked Samson, he pulled a flask of whiskey out of a bag. "You ain't one a them prohibitionists, are ya? I'd like a drink and I don't like to drink alone." He took a long pull and passed the flask to Oleta. The burning whiskey left her choking and coughing.

"Take 'er easy, Oleta. Here, try it again, but don't take so much this time."

Oleta could feel the warmth spreading, along with a strange buzzing sensation. After the third swallow Oleta's head began to swim. When Burl handed her the flask again she shook her head. Burl tucked it in his saddlebag and began nuzzling her neck again while running his hands down her sides and around her bottom. She thought vaguely that she should stop him, but she didn't really want to. After a few heady minutes he held her at arm's length and looked her up and down.

"Damn! You are about as purty a girl as I ever seen." As he said this one of his hands slid from her waist up to her breast and he leaned down and kissed her cleavage.

"Hey, how about we go for a ride? What do ya say?"

Oleta knew exactly what she *should* say, but dizzily heard herself saying instead, "Sure. I love to ride in the moonlight."

Burl saddled Samson, then lifted Oleta up and mounted behind her, tucking her securely in front of him. They sauntered along the edge of the river for half a mile or so, then veered off into the sagebrush toward a distant cottonwood tree. All along the way, Burl kissed her hair and neck and ran his free hand over her breasts and down her thigh. She felt an electrifying thrill course through her and all she wanted was to have him keep doing it.

Burl pulled Samson up near the isolated cottonwood tree and dismounted, reaching up for her afterwards. He took another swallow of whiskey and handed her the flask then removed his bedroll and spread it out under the tree.

Oleta tried vaguely to reason with herself, but her head was so fuzzy all she could think was, *what the hell, if Mae West can do it, why not me?* She took another swallow of whiskey and looked at him, his tight jeans bent over the bedroll, and decided she just didn't give a damn.

Emboldened by the whiskey and more than a little drunk, she wrapped her arms around him and began licking his ear. He dropped to the blanket taking her with him.

* * * * *

"Hell, darlin', you shoulda told me this was your first time. I'da been gentler with ya." Burl cupped her breasts with both his hands and kissed a nipple. His speech was slurred from the whiskey.

"It's ok. I liked it. I'm not supposed to, though, am I? But I did, even if it did hurt some." Oleta was sore, but with her head swimming from the whiskey and his honeyed words in her ear she shed all pretense. "I can't believe I'm laying here under the stars buck naked with a buck naked cowboy. Damn!" She stretched like a cat and leaned over him, resting one hand on his thigh.

"Want to do it again?"

Oleta tiptoed into Cass's house shortly before dawn. She was terrified that she would wake someone while she was sneaking up the stairs, but managed to get into Cass's room without being heard. She was still feeling woozy from the alcohol when she passed out next to Cass. The next morning she was violently ill and could hardly walk. Oleta was afraid Cass's mother would figure out she had been drinking, but she was so worried about Cass that she hardly even noticed Oleta. Oleta was sure that Joe suspected she'd been drinking though; that stony silence all the way home was more than worry about Cass. She felt guilty about the night before, but at the same time she couldn't stop thinking about it and smiling. Besides, she would never see him again, so it was just her wild little romantic fling, a one-time thing to look back on when she was an old lady with ten kids. She vowed never to tell anyone, except maybe Cass.

* * * * *

"Soooo, Cass?" she asked, "are you shocked?"

Cass stared at Oleta.

"You are shocked, I can tell. But please don't judge me, Cass. I couldn't stand that."

"I'm not, Oleta, honest. But you can't ever tell anyone else. You know that, don't you? What would they think? Oh my God! What if you'd gotten pregnant?"

"I don't think you can even get pregnant the first time. Besides, it was just a one-night wild fling, like in the movies. I'm never going to see him again, so no one will ever know but you. But that's not all. There's something else I want to tell you, before your mom makes me leave."

Cass's eyes widened.

"No, nothing like that, just something that I'm afraid you won't like and I don't want you to get mad at me. I don't ever want to lose my best friend again. But you're going to hear about this anyway and I want to tell you the real story before you hear a bunch of gossip.

"You know how we always go to the fair together? Well, I was wandering around with my cotton candy, feeling lonely and missing you, when I ran into Clete Algood in the cattle barn. Well, we got to talking and flirting and you know how he's got them blue eyes. One thing led to another and before I knew it we was making out right there in the straw. You know how I've had sort of a crush on him for years and, well, it turns out he's been hot for me too. The thing is, I've gone out with him every night he's been in town since the fair."

"But he's engaged to Annie! You didn't . . ."

"No, I already told you. That was just a one-time thing. And he's not. Engaged, I mean. They're going steady, that's all, and he's going to break up with her as soon as he sees her again."

"Oleta, this isn't right. They aren't just going steady. They're practically engaged, everybody knows that. You remember how they were at that party, how he looked at her? And even if they are only going steady, that's still not right! And if he wants to break up with her, why doesn't he do it instead of sneaking around?"

Oleta's voice began to break as she became increasingly defensive. "Cause he don't want to be cruel. She's crazy about him and she lives with his sister, so everything's kind of complicated. He wants to wait until he can tell her in person, let her down gentle-like, like he should."

"But Oleta, how can you trust someone who'd do that to a girl he's known all his life? How do you know he won't toss you aside the minute some other pretty girl comes along?"

Oleta opened her mouth as if to reply, then sat next to Cass and put her arms around her. She laid her head on her shoulder and her eyes filled. "Cass," she said, "I know I ought to stay away from him. Maybe he won't break up with Annie, I don't know. But when he holds me and tells me how pretty I am and how he wants to be with me every minute of the day, well hell, how can I say no? I ain't never going to be a cute little blonde like Annie, but he wants to be with me. Me. Me with my big hips and my big breasts and my big laugh. Not meek little say-nothing Annie." She uttered these last words through a partially suppressed sob.

Cass sighed and smoothed Oleta's hair. "Shhh. I didn't mean to make you cry. Maybe you're right. You know him better than I do. But be careful. Promise me?" Oleta nodded. "Does everybody know about this?"

Oleta perked up. "Well sure! We been to the movies the last two weekends. Couldn't tell you what we saw though, not where we were sitting in the corner seats in the back of the balcony. When he kisses me my heart melts right down into my shoes. One night in the balcony he had my bra all undone when the lights come on. We had to wait till everyone left so I could fix it." When Cass looked alarmed, Oleta reassured her. "It's only a little petting in the balcony. I won't let him go no further."

Oleta nattered on about how he was always bursting into song, even making up verses about her brown eyes and singing it to the tune of "Back in the Saddle Again." Every date ended in a parked car out near the reservoir. Oleta talked about Clete until Cass's mother told her it was time for her to go home.

(August 1940-March 1941)

After she left Cass could not rest. She knew Oleta was so hungry for love that she would do anything to get it and she was terrified for her. Terrified, but dead tired too. She finally fell into a fitful sleep, awaking in the middle of the night, anxious and worried as she mulled over everything Oleta had confided in her.

She didn't see Oleta again until she started back to school in late September, almost a month later. Oleta had written two or three times a week for the first few weeks, even calling once from the drug store pay phone bubbling, absolutely giddy about a locket Clete had bought her. She had been in town for the afternoon, but didn't have time to come see Cass because she and Clete were going to the matinee. All she could talk about was Clete, Clete, Clete. Cass didn't dare ask if he had talked to Annie yet, but it was the one thing she was dying to know. The morning Cass walked into the school for the first time that fall she hadn't heard from Oleta for nearly two weeks. Oleta had not answered the letter she had sent her the week before and Cass was worried. She was mobbed by well-wishers hugging her and welcoming her back.

Arch had come by the house to walk her to school, but he had to get to auto shop early, so Cass took her books and meandered back outside to wait for Oleta's bus. The morning was nearly perfect, dry and mild, the azure sky streaked with wisps of cottony clouds. The three large chestnuts across the street had begun to turn gold and the small maple on the front lawn was a vivid red. Cass waited impatiently until the route #3 bus finally pulled up minutes before the bell was set to ring. Student after student greeted her as they disembarked and hurried to class. The last one out of the bus was Oleta.

It was obvious that something was wrong. Oleta was folded into herself in a way unique to her, her eyes haunted and lifeless, her face pale, her shoulders hunched. Cass took her arm and pulled her aside.

"Oleta, what's wrong?"

"I can't talk, not now. I'll start crying again." She set her jaw and shook off the tears. "Let's just go to class. I need you to help me pretend everything is ok. Please Cass!" The desperation in her voice was chilling.

"Sure. We'll win an academy award. Put a smile on; we can do this." Cass watched as Oleta transformed, twisting her face into a smile and straightening her body, much as she had at the Merc that day in June, and they entered the school arm in arm as the first bell rang.

Arch was not happy when Cass told him she was going to eat alone with Oleta and slammed his books on the desk in a rare display of temper before sulking off to join his friends. Cass and Oleta grabbed their lunches and walked to the far corner of the field out behind the school. Oleta began crying before she even sat down.

"Clete broke up with me. He went over to Boise to tell Annie about us and when he came back, he was changed. I could tell right away that something was wrong. We drove over to Bully Creek to this place we always go to and he told me that he couldn't do it, that he thought he could, but when he was with her, he just wanted to stay with her. He said that she made his heart sing. I asked him if he loved her and he said he wasn't sure, but I know he does. He said it wasn't fair to me and that it had all been a mistake. He said he really liked me, but we probably shouldn't go out anymore until he figured it all out. And he wouldn't hardly even touch me."

"Oh, Oleta, I'm so sorry."

"It's worse than that. I lied to you. I told you that the thing with Burl was a one-time thing, but it wasn't. I done it with Clete, too, at the fair. I don't know what got into me. It was like I was drunk on his sweet-talking or something. After that I told him we couldn't do that again and we come close, but I

only gave in a couple of other times out at the reservoir. I'm
so nuts about him I can't seem to stop myself."

Oleta began to sob. "And I'm pregnant."

Cass felt as though she had swallowed a fishing weight.
The day that had dawned so radiantly beautiful suddenly
seemed as dreary as a rainy day in winter. In the distance
they heard the school bell. Cass held Oleta until she could
get her composure, then made arrangements for her to stay in
town the next night on the pretext of a school project. With
leaden feet they trudged the long yards back into the school.

* * * * *

It took two weeks for Oleta to screw up the courage to
tell Clete. She didn't even know where he was exactly, as he
moved around from ranch to ranch, depending on where he
was needed. Eventually she wrote him a letter care of the last
ranch where she knew he had been working telling him she
really needed to see him. He went to her place that weekend and they drove out to their special place near Bully Creek
Siphon.

The minute he turned off the car he started kissing her
and pushing her down on the seat. She thought that meant
he had changed his mind and responded passionately to his
advances. After it was over, though, he started the car as if
to take her home. She asked him to wait, then started crying.
He put his arm around her, kind of loosely as if he were in a
hurry to get home. By the time she told him about the baby
she was crying so hard she couldn't even see his face. He
clenched the steering wheel with both hands and stared off
into space then told her he needed to think. He walked off into
the sagebrush and didn't come back for half an hour. When he
finally returned she thought it looked as though he had been
crying as much as she had. His eyes were red and his face
blotchy. But when he got in that car he put his arm around

her and told her, "Well, doll, I think we better get married,
don't you?"

*****

Clete and Oleta were married by the justice of the peace
on the last day of October. Arch and Cass stood with them,
but nobody else was there, not even their parents. She quit
school and never went back.

Clete put the money he had saved into the hardscrabble
quarter section he had had his eye on and they moved into
a tiny two-room shack next to the original stone house that
was on the property. She was out there alone most of the
time while he worked as much as he could on some of the
big farms and ranches out Juntura way, sometimes as far as
Jordan Valley. Often he would be gone for a week or two at a
time and she'd be stranded on the silent farm with no phone
and no car, the nearest neighbor miles away. Even when he
was home he worked nearly all the time, building a barn and
hen house, clearing sagebrush, and preparing to add another
two rooms onto the house. Oleta never complained, even to
Cass, who got Arch to drive her out for a visit a couple of
times. While Clete poured himself into the farm, Oleta fixed
up the house and sewed baby blankets and clothes from the
inexpensive end pieces she bought at the Merc.

On the few times they did get together Oleta chattered incessantly about Clete and their plans, how she wanted a May
Day baby who would slide on out like it was coming down a
maypole. But Clark wasn't any May Day baby, not even close.
He was born on the 27th of March. And he was a nice big
healthy eight-pound boy.

Chapter 8
Jean, Cass, and Opal

(August 1971)

Cass started when a hand was placed on her shoulder.

"Go home, Cass. You were up half the night with us yesterday. You must be bushed. Aunt Opal is staying with me until Clark comes and Mom will need you tomorrow. Where did this come from?" She pointed to a cloth-covered basket sitting on the coffee table next to a pile of magazines.

"Leroy brought that by while you were in visiting your dad. He said to give you his best and that he'd check in tomorrow."

Jean lifted the cloth. "Zucchini bread and melon slices. That was sweet of the Fulmers." She picked up a slice of bread. "Do you want some?"

"No thanks. Save what you don't eat for Opal, and Clark when he comes." Cass sat up and rubbed her tweaked neck. "I'm definitely feeling my age tonight, that's for sure. Maybe I will go home and get some sleep. I'll be more use if I'm not half dead. How did that go with Opal?"

Jean thought of the way Opal had looked when she saw Clete. Her eyes had filled when she reached out to touch Clete's hand, but she had set her jaw firmly and had held back the tears. Arm in arm they had stood next to his bed in silence. Jean had found it surprisingly soothing to be there with her.

"Good, actually. Kind of comforting, or at least a lot better than when I went in by myself." Jean realized that she had never considered how Opal might be feeling since she and her brother had never been all that close. Now that she thought about it, she wondered if that was because he pushed her away and not because of Opal. *And he is her only brother,* she thought. Opal covered it the best she could, but Jean could tell that she was suffering in there. "I think she only had me go in with her to help me, not for her. Am I even making sense?"

"More than you know, sweetie, more than you know." Cass started to stand and fell back into the chair. "Damned knees aren't worth a rat's ass anymore."

Jean hugged Cass tightly. "You aren't seriously going to abandon me to Aunt Opal are you," she asked, only half joking.

"If I do you might discover there is more to Opal than you thought. Don't get me wrong, she acts like she has a rod up her ass half the time, but there's another side to her that not many people know about. I love your mom like a sister, but she can barely take care of herself half the time. She's sure not much use in a crisis. Times like this, you need people like Opal."

Cass reached over and took Jean's hand. "When my Archie died I was pretty bad off. That was 1945. Horrible, horrible year. In January of that year both my parents died within three weeks of each other, Dad from a heart attack, Mom from cancer. Then, not a month later, my brother Joe was killed in France. I had moved back in with my folks in 1942 when Archie, my husband, was captured by the Japanese, so I was dragging around in that huge house, sick with grief and worrying myself nigh to death about Archie. The only thing keeping me going was thinking about the war ending and Archie coming home. When the Germans surrendered I knew it was only a matter of time until the Japanese followed suit. That hope was pretty much all that got me up in the mornings. Then one month followed another and the war dragged on and on, month after month. I got the telegram the same day we got the news that the Japanese had surrendered, August 14th, 1945. The worst day of my life. All over town people were whooping and hollering, pouring into the streets celebrating. And my life had just ended.

"I was so filled up with grief that I didn't know how I was going to put one foot in front of the other. After the funeral I holed up in my bed. I didn't comb my hair, hardly ate, didn't go to work. Your mom came by when she could, but she would start lamenting and I'd end up trying to comfort her. Plus, she had those three little boys with her. Clark was always a sweet gentle little thing, but those twins were hellions, adorable, but out of control, like Oleta. Seeing those little ones was a reminder of everything that I was never going to have and it was pure pain to have them there. Of course I didn't know then that they . . ."

Cass paused. "Anyway, I couldn't see much point in going on living. As long as I was asleep, I didn't have to face the emptiness. About a month or so after the funeral, Opal showed up one morning. She let herself in and fixed an enormous breakfast – biscuits, bacon, scrambled eggs, coffee. Then she came upstairs and dragged me out of bed and forced me to come down and eat it. To this day I have no idea how she did that. She was a little bit of a thing, couldn't have been ninety pounds back then, but she was like a bulldozer. She sat me at the table and kept shoving forkfuls of food at me like I was a baby. I finally took the fork away and fed myself just to get her to stop. After that she marched me into the bathroom and made me take a shower and wash my hair. She ran the water and would have undressed me herself if I hadn't co-operated. And I wasn't particularly nice to her either; I swore at her, called her names, but she kept at me like she was stone deaf.

She even made me go outside with her to tend to the garden. It was like I had no will of my own. She stayed until she had watched me eat my dinner, then went on home.

"The next day she was back again, first thing in the morning, and the next and the next. She kept it up until she came one morning and I was sitting at the kitchen table, showered and dressed, eating a bowl of oatmeal. The only way I could get her to stop was by commencing to live. After that, I started to heal. It was slow, but she put me on the road."

"I wonder why mom never told me about that. I don't think I've ever heard her say one good thing about Aunt Opal."

"I don't think she knows. I didn't tell her. It was between Opal and me. I don't know why that is, but it is. There's a whole lot more to Opal than you give her credit for. You never knew your Grandmother Algood, but she had a massive stroke when Opal was only about 15. Couldn't talk, couldn't walk, couldn't even feed herself. Clete and Cloris had just left home and it fell to Opal to nurse her as well as take over running the household. Your grandfather was pretty much useless. Opal was nurse, cook, housekeeper, and moral support to her dad – all when most kids are just worried about impressing some cute boy in English class. Her mother lingered on like that for nearly two years. She's got a spine of steel, Opal does. People aren't always who we think they are, that's all I'm saying. And the same goes for your mom. When this is all behind us I want you to come over and we'll have a heart to heart about your mom. Maybe you and Mae both."

"That would be wonderful, Cass. Thank you."

After Cass left Jean stretched out on the couch with her magazine, but her mind couldn't focus on it. After reading the same page three times, she tossed the magazine aside and stared at the sickly walls, chewing her way from one fingernail to the next, watching the clock and willing someone, anyone, to walk into the empty, lifeless room.

Half an hour later Opal finally emerged from the ICU, black

smears beneath her eyes, her face puffy and blotchy, and burst into tears. Jean held her awkwardly as Opal wept. After a few minutes, Jean helped her to a chair and brought her tissues.

Opal blew her nose and choked out her words spasmodically. "He looks so, so . . wrong. All those tubes and machines! He's always hated doctors and hospitals, wouldn't even go to the doctor when he crushed his hand in the cattle chute, not until Oleta got Leroy over there to talk some sense into him. He would hate this." Opal dabbed at her eyes and pulled a compact out of her purse. "Mercy! Aren't I a sight?" She sniffed, forcing a half smile. "I came here to comfort you, and just look at me."

Jean stroked her hand. "That's all right, Aunt Opal. It's a comfort having you here. This must be really rough for you too. He's the only one you have left in your family."

"Well, no dear – there's still our sister Cloris, you know. She ought to be here. I'll never stop hoping and praying that someday she'll come back to us. I just know she will."

Jean chewed on her thumbnail as she chewed on Opal's words. "Aunt Opal, what happened to Aunt Cloris? Dad would never talk about her and the only thing we ever got out of Mom was that she thought she was too good for the rest of us, so good riddance. Cass told me that she and Dad used to be close, but that's about all she'd say. I've never even seen her."

Opal, who had almost completely restored her face, quickly assumed her usual brusque manner. She closed the compact with a decisive snap and dropped it back in her orange purse. "Jeannie, I'll tell you what I can, but I don't fully understand it myself."

Opal sketched the outlines of a relationship that had gone sour. When Clete and Cloris were kids it was always the two of them, joined at the hip like twins often are. Opal was just the irritating little sister. Their close relationship came to an abrupt end when Clete married Oleta instead of Cloris's friend. He had been going with Cloris's best friend Annie since they were in high school, but dropped her without warning and married Oleta instead. Cloris couldn't ever seem to get over it for some reason, which was a ridiculous over-reaction, according to Opal. Cloris didn't speak to him for years. She and Annie lived together in Boise, and Cloris never came home without bringing her. After the twins died they patched things up and she was a real support to him when he was grieving. And then she disappeared.

No one heard from her for over a year. Opal finally drove over to Boise and tracked her down. She knew she was working in a bank so she went from bank to bank until she found her. Cloris refused to discuss Clete then or in any of the years since, and she never stepped foot in Vale again. About the time Jean was born Cloris moved to Portland. Her boss at the bank in Boise told Opal how to get hold of her or she might never have found her.

"If I didn't write her every month or two, and call every Christmas, my sister would slip away from us for good. It's a real grief to me. I called her three times yesterday to tell her about your dad but she's got one of those new-fangled answering machines and I don't even know if she's listening to it. I might have to call when I get home today and wake her up. Sometimes I think everything just went to hell, forgive my French, when Jimmy and Joey died."

"That's something else no one will talk about. All I know is that they died in an accident, but I don't know anything about what happened to them, and they were my brothers."

"Well, Jeannie. There are stories in this life that can be too darned painful to tell. But you're right. You ought to know."

Chapter 9
The Twins

(August 24, 1946)

Saturday August 24th was as close to perfection as an August day in far eastern Oregon can be. On Friday, the searing heat that had enshrouded the valley for nearly a month gave way to unseasonably mild temperatures and the thermometer barely topped eighty even during the hottest part of the day. When Clete went out to the chicken coop to select a young rooster for the picnic, a mild breeze caressed the parched trees, a profound change from the merciless string of scorching hot days they had endured for weeks. Only the rustling of leaves and the chattering of magpies fractured the calm.

Opal, who had arrived early to help Oleta, had been bustling about the kitchen all morning, prattling as incessantly as one of the magpies. The rolls were rising nicely while a kettle of water heated on the stove to loosen the chicken's feathers. For the past several minutes she had been meticulously separating eggs for the cake, slowly pouring the yolks from shell to shell as though they were made of gold.

"I think we ought to leave the cake here and have it when we get back from the river, don't you? Yesterday was cooler and all, but the chocolate could melt and it'd be a blamed shame. Harry just loves chocolate cake. Poor man. Can you imagine? Getting the chicken pox at his age! I hated to leave him at home all alone, but he said he only wanted to sleep all day anyway. When he gets well I'm going to make him a seven-layer red velvet cake. What do you think?"

Oleta, who had been surly since Opal arrived, scowled. She looked up from dicing the potatoes for the potato salad, holding the knife off to one side. "What I think is that you're never going to get this cake made if you keep pussyfooting around with those eggs. Good Lord!"

She commenced chopping, even more aggressively than before, when she was nearly knocked into the stove by Jimmy and Joey, who tore through the kitchen squealing and chasing each other. She caught her fall with her free arm and the knife clattered to the floor.

"Hells bells! I nearly burned myself. Outside, both of you! Clark, go watch your brothers!" Clark had been sitting quietly at the table watching her work, as was his way. The twins raced out the front door, but Clark stayed at the table, hoping to be ignored.

"Didn't I just tell you to go watch your brothers? Out!"

"Ah, Mama. Do I hafta?" Clark lifted his chocolate eyes hopefully to his mother, but she just waved a damp hand at him in a shooing motion.

"Git! Don't make me tell you again!"

Reluctantly, Clark followed his brothers, who had gathered around the chopping block to watch Clete decapitate the rooster. Opal, working at the table, gave up carrying on a conversation with Oleta and watched the little boys through the screened window.

"Now, stand back you two." Deftly, Clete held the rooster's legs with one hand and, swinging the ax, lopped off the head. Squirting blood, the headless chicken twisted and writhed in a macabre dance before flopping lifeless in the dust. The two little boys watched round-eyed, thumbs in their mouths, until the chicken stopped twitching; then, giggling and shrieking, they chased one another around and around the barnyard pretending to be headless chickens. Clark picked up a stick and poked the chicken a few times.

Clete tousled Clark's coarse unruly hair. "Hey, Buddy, did Mom kick you outside with those two rascals again? How would you like to help me pluck the chicken after I scald it?" Clark's eyes lit up in the glow of his father's attention. Nudging Clark's hand with his head, Bob, the black and white mongrel, begged for attention too. While Clete went in to scald the chicken to loosen the feathers, Clark threw a stick for Bob, ignoring Joey and Jimmy as they tormented a yellow and white barn cat.

Clete came back out dangling the scalded chicken in one hand and gathered up all three boys. He took them out into the field next to the house where he could keep his eye on the twins while he plucked the chicken. Deftly he pulled fists full of pinfeathers while Clark tugged tentatively at some of the larger wing feathers. The twins busied themselves making dandelion and feather bouquets. Clete had barely finished gutting the chicken when a dark gray Ford turned into the lane.

"Clark, you think you can run this in to your Mom?" Clete lifted Clark over the fence into the yard and handed him the naked chicken. Clark gingerly grasped a foot in each hand and walked solemnly and awkwardly toward the house as though entrusted with a great honor.

Clete wiped his hands on his pants and waited motionlessly as the car approached. For several years after his marriage he had not seen Annie, but as Karl had become more withdrawn she had come to Vale as often as gas rationing would allow. They no longer acted awkward when they met, but this was the first time that either she or Cloris had come out to Clete and Oleta's farm. That they were here today was due to Opal, who had lobbied relentlessly for more time together with all three siblings. What better time, she had insisted, than the twins' third birthday? Worn down, Cloris had finally agreed, but on the condition that Annie come too, since Annie was coming to Vale with her for the weekend.

Clete sauntered over to the car as Annie slid out of the passenger seat, dazzling in a pale blue sundress, her hair swept up in a loose ponytail. The twins darted towards the car, tumbling over one another to get to the steering wheel.

Inside the house, Opal closed the oven door and untied her apron. "If you don't mind, I think I'll go on out and say "howdy". The screen door slammed behind her, but she paused for a minute to re-open the door for Clark, who struggled with the plucked chicken.

She heard his voice as she left the yard. "Look Mama. I did it almost all by myself!"

A few minutes later, Oleta sent him back out. The screen door slammed behind him as he emerged from the house and ran out the front gate to join Clete. Karl and Clete were leaning against the car, talking. Annie had both Jimmy and Joey on her lap as they pretended to steer, and Cloris sat in the passenger seat with the door ajar, finishing a cigarette.

"Cloris, Annie! "Opal called. "Isn't it the most beautiful day? Me and Oleta have been cooking up a storm. If Harry were here this day would be perfect."

Cloris looked at Annie and groaned, loud enough that Opal could hear. "Lord, give me strength!" Annie's tinkling laugh reached Clete, who watched as Cloris stepped out of the car. She wore a white blouse tied at her waist baring her midriff and a pair of khaki shorts. Her long muscled legs were deeply tanned and bare to the thigh.

"Jesus H. Christ!" Clete said. "What the hell are you wearing? Did you forget to get dressed today?"

Opal, who like Annie wore a cotton print dress, pursed her lips. "Are you sure that's appropriate, Cloris? You know, around the kids?"

Annie, who had disengaged herself from the boys, glided gracefully from the car and startled everyone by coming to Cloris's defense. "I like it. I think she looks pretty." After she spoke Annie reddened and shot Cloris a quick smile before looking down at the ground.

Cloris stuck her head in the car. "Hey boys, what do you think of your Aunt Cloris? Do I embarrass you?" The boys glanced at her momentarily and went back to fighting over the steering wheel.

Cloris turned to Opal and Clete. "Just for the record, I don't give a rat's ass what you think, so unless you want me to turn around and go home right now, knock it off." She looked directly at Opal and ground her cigarette butt into the dirt with a cork-toed sandal. "And don't even think about saying anything about my smoking."

Clete grumbled that he was going to see if Oleta needed help and headed for the house. Opal mumbled an apology. After Clete left, Karl slid into the vacant passenger seat. His soft voice could barely be heard, but whatever he said to the twins delighted them. Squealing and giggling, Jimmy and Joey clambered onto his lap. Annie knelt down and started a conversation with Clark who was half hiding behind the car tracing pictures on the dusty fender with his finger.

From the house Oleta's shrill voice rang in the quiet air. "Left me here to fry up this goddamned chicken while you lollygagged around. You're too busy flirting with your old girlfriend to lift a finger to help your own wife!"

"Keep your voice down, goddamn it! Did you ever think maybe I like looking at a woman who hasn't turned into a damned cow?"

"Hey, whose birthday is it?" Cloris called, opening the driver's door and leaning into the car, tickling Jimmy. Joey joined his brother in an assault on their aunt and Karl slipped out of the car. Annie, pale and frowning, joined Karl, lacing one arm through his. Soon the shrieks of the two three-year olds drowned out any sounds from the house. Opening the gate, Opal strode into the yard, announcing loudly that she thought she ought to check on the cake.

It was past noon before the six adults and three children finally started out across the back pasture and on through the greasewood, the cheat grass swishing and rustling as they walked. Joey and Jimmy, running ahead with Bob, chased a butterfly. Clark hovered near Oleta, dragging a stick over the ruts, gouging up hoary chunks of alkaline clay and clouds of dust. A cold beer, the pervasive aroma of deep-fried chicken, the temperate day, all had restored Clete's festive mood. As he and Karl hiked, following closely behind the twins, his stomach began rumbling and gurgling so loudly that they were sent into spasms of laughter. The rumbling was so loud that even Cloris and Annie, who were lagging behind them, heard it and started giggling.

Clete turned around and walked backwards, talking to Annie and Cloris. "Well hell, what do you expect? I have to carry this fried chicken all the way to the river on an empty stomach. It's more than a man should have to bear!" He then did something that Opal couldn't remember him doing for years – he started singing.

"I'm a Yankee Doodle dandy, Yankee Doodle do or die. . ."

Cloris draped one arm around his neck and the other around Annie's and joined him, slightly off-key. *"A real live nephew of my Uncle Sam . . . "*

Behind them, Opal and Oleta brought up the rear, Opal falling over herself trying to cheer Oleta, whose black mood plodded along with them.

"Isn't it great to hear them singing together again like they used to do when they were in high school? I wonder what they were all laughing about?"

Oleta stopped walking and stared at Opal, as though she were looking at a locust. "What the hell do you think they're laughing about, Opal? Hells bells! Could it be how nice it is to be together again, thanks to Clete's dear little sister? Or maybe they're laughing about how funny it is that Clete's fat cow of a wife is so stupid she can't see what's going on right in front of her nose." Oleta's set jaw quivered.

"Oh no, hon, you've got it all wrong. They're just laughing over old times, that's all. That thing between them was over with a long, long time ago. Don't you go worrying about that." She hurried to catch up with Oleta. "Clete loves you, you know that. He's just a little thoughtless sometimes. You oughtn't put yourself down that way. You're full-figured, that's all. Look at me, nothing but a stick figure, no curves at all, but you're all woman. And you're a good mother too — look at how little Clark there adores you – you must be doing something right."

Oleta, wiping her eyes with her arm, refused to even look at Opal. Choking back tears she looked down at Clark, who had stayed right by her side. Idly she stroked his hair, then shaded her eyes and looked off into the distance. "Now where did those two boys get to?"

"Clete," she yelled. "I can't see Joey and Jimmy."

Clete cupped his hands and called to the boys. When there was no response he called Bob, who darted out from behind a willow tree that leaned into the bank a hundred yards ahead. By this time they could hear shrieking and splashing.

"Joey, Jimmy! Get away from that river until we get there or I'll tan your hides!" Clete had started to jog toward the stream when the boys emerged from the willow with sticks they had been using to splash the water. Clete slowed again to a walk, keeping his eye on the boys until the group reached the river.

This isolated spot was a favorite one for the family, as it was readily accessible via the fields. By late August the water level had dropped so much that parts of the main river were no more than a foot deep, good for the children to wade in. Two craggy cottonwoods grew close together, shading the bank, and Clete had cleared a wide swath of greasewood and sagebrush, creating a sort of alkaline beach. Sometime before they had moved to the farm another cottonwood that had stood as part of the grove had fallen and now served as a makeshift bench for the picnickers.

The two men found a small pool under a willow to stash the beer and sodas and waded out into the shallow stream with the three boys.

Hearing the boys' gleeful giggling seemed to leaven Oleta's spirits. As she and Opal laid out the blankets and food she visibly relaxed.

Cloris kicked off her sandals and walked to the water's edge, fishing out a beer. "Anyone else want a beer? Oleta? How about you, Opal? Or do you still belong to the temperance union?"

"Damned right I want one," Oleta replied. Opal, who was bending over to remove her shoes, waved her hand dismissively.

Annie leaned over to Opal and whispered, "Don't let it bother you. She doesn't tease people she doesn't care about."

"Opal?" Cloris held up a Grape Nehi. Opal nodded.

Oleta had two good swallows before the three little boys came tearing out of the water begging to eat, followed by the laughing men, water dripping from their rolled up cuffs. The next half hour was filled with lazy conversation, the crunch of crisp fried chicken, and the scraping of forks on plates. The twins turned up their noses at the potato salad, but ate a drumstick each before they picked up sticks and started playing in the greasewood. Bob stretched out in the shade of the willow, panting. Clark sat at water's edge making mud pies.

Oleta got up to follow the boys, but Clete stopped her. "Let them play – it's their birthday."

He called to the boys. "Joey, Jimmy. You stay close now, you hear."

"They're going to get ticks, Clete."

Clete stretched out full length on the blanket, lying on his back, ignoring her. Oleta sat back down. Opal half reclined on the next blanket, leaning against the log. Cloris lit another cigarette while Annie used her as a back support, leaning against her, legs stretched out with her skirt spread like the wings of a butterfly. The pungent odor of burning tobacco wafted through the air and mingled with the oily camphor smell of the greasewood.

"Hey, Sis. Toss me the pack."

Clete rolled over on his side, his back to Oleta, lit a cigarette, and looked directly at Annie. "Remember that day we went fishing up on the Burnt River? It was a pretty day like this one, but kind of cold – May, I think it was. We were out there all day and didn't catch a damned fish, not that we tried all that hard. You was wearing a blue sweater the exact same color as the sky— and your eyes." Clete smiled wistfully as he remembered. "We was horsing around and you turned your ankle, remember? I had to carry you better than a mile back to the truck. Didn't much mind, though, not with you in my arms."

Annie blushed a deep scarlet and abruptly sat up. Behind Clete, Oleta noticeably bristled. Cloris scowled at her brother and opened her mouth as if to speak, but instead made a smacking sound with her lips and stood up, holding her hand out to Annie to help her rise.

"Annie and me are going for a little walk, see if we can work off some of Oleta's good fried chicken."

Oleta didn't say a word, but her eyes brimmed with tears as she grabbed a stack of plates and stomped down to the river to rinse them. Karl gathered up the spoons and forks and did the same. Clete rolled onto his back and covered his face with his hat. Opal ached for Oleta, and was furious with her brother for ruining the moment so thoroughly.

Silence screamed in the clearing. Oleta slowly, meticulously scrubbed each plate, then carried the stack back to the blanket and set it down hard next to Clete. He flinched, but did not open his eyes.

"Where are the boys?" Her eyes swept the empty field, as she turned in a circle. "Jimmy! Joey!" There was no response.

She called again. Again there was no response. "Clete, I don't know where the boys are." Clete jumped up and began calling. His voice reverberated in the motionless air, but still there was no reply.

He motioned to Oleta and Opal. "You look upstream, I'll head down. By this time, Karl had already started downstream, calling in his soft but clear voice, searching under willows, scanning the river. Minutes later, he shouted, a heart-rending cry.

Clete reached him in time to receive the small limp body he had pulled from the deep pool eddying under a willow cluster. Immediately after handing Jimmy to Clete, Karl plunged back into the pool, sweeping his arms under water until he found Joey, his red plaid shirt snagged on a craggy root extending from the bank.

Opal had started running when she heard Karl's inhuman cry. She arrived in time to catch Oleta when she collapsed. The two little boys lay on their stomachs, Karl pushing and pounding on Joey's back, Clete, his face rent with grief, doing the same to Jimmy. As Cloris and Annie came running up, Jimmy coughed, water and vomit spilling from his mouth, and took several ragged breaths. Joey remained motionless, his lips the same cerulean blue as the sky, his small body as still as the inert air.

Frantic, Clete hoisted Jimmy onto his shoulder and shouted at Karl. "Bring Joey! We have to get them to the hospital." He tore across the field toward the house, Bob barking at his heels, Jimmy's unconscious form jolting as he ran. Immediately behind him Karl followed with Joey, racing across the snow-white alkaline fields to where the car waited at the house, a mile in the distance.

Frozen in horror, Opal took a second to register the sound

coming from behind her, then turned to see Clark, covered in mud, staring at her, his mahogany eyes round with fear. She immediately pulled him to her. "It'll be alright, sweetheart. Your brothers had a little accident and your daddy is taking them to the doctor. Your mommy's upset, but Aunt Opal will take care of you.

Annie and Cloris were kneeling on the riverbank trying to calm Oleta, who held her arms to her chest and rocked, sobbing hysterically. "It's my fault. I should have been watching them. Oh God! My boys! My boys! Oh, God!"

Opal, Clark clinging to her skirt, called as calmly as she could to Annie and Cloris. "Annie, come take Clark. Cloris, there's a tractor road that goes out to the back of the Oxman's spread not far from where the river makes a sharp bend, about a quarter mile north of here. Go get your car and drive around and meet us. You might have to drive across the fields the last little bit. Watch for the track right before the Oxman's place. Annie and me will get Oleta and Clark as close as we can to the road."

Cloris tore across the field. Annie sat down by Clark and took him in her lap, stroking his hair and soothing him with her gentle voice. Opal knelt on the ground facing Oleta and took hold of her upper arms staring hard into her eyes.

"Oleta, look at me. You can cry all you want later. You can worry about whose fault it is later. Right now we have to get you to the hospital to be with your boys. Do you hear me, Oleta?" Opal kept on until she was able to get Oleta to her feet. Struggling to support Oleta's bulk with her tiny frame, she dragged her toward the road. Annie carried Clark, who clung to her neck sobbing as they stumbled towards the bend in the river. They watched a billowing dust cloud announcing Cloris's approach and tumbled into her car the moment it jounced to a stop atop a small sagebrush.

When they arrived in Ontario thirty minutes later a grim-faced Karl was pacing the waiting room where Clete was slumped, his head in his hands. When he saw Oleta he began to sob, chest heaving, and they clung to one another, two broken parents both blaming themselves, both inconsolable.

(August 1971)

Opal cleared her throat and daubed at her eyes before continuing. "Joey was already dead, never showed a sign of life from the time he was pulled out of that river. Jimmy was alive, though, and we huddled together in this same waiting room all night long, but he never regained consciousness. Died the next morning. I'll never forget when I drove up to their house that next day. I had to get some clothes for Clark — he stayed with us for a few weeks. Walking into that kitchen and seeing that chocolate cake sitting on the table waiting for those two little boys to come blow out the candles near to broke my heart."

Opal looked around. "That was twenty-five years ago and the walls are still the same vomit green. That's real cheerful, isn't it?"

"Thank you, Aunt Opal. I never knew this. No one would talk about it. I can't imagine what that must have been like for Mom and Dad. It's no wonder we weren't allowed to go anywhere near that river. Being here again must bring all that horror back for Mom."

Opal looked over at the paper bag sitting next to Jean. "Do you think you could spare one of those silly candy bars of yours? You know, I've never actually eaten one of those things – they always looked so ridiculous." Jean handed her the potato shaped bar and Opal began to peel back the wrapper.

"I think I could use some silly today – might even steal that *MAD Magazine* Will sent you." She took a dainty bite, bits of coconut scattering over her dress and down her neck. "Mmm. Not bad," she said, sinking her teeth into the squishy middle.

Jean squeezed Opal's moist hand. "Have some zucchini bread too. I think I'll go sit with Dad for a while."

She started toward the ICU then turned back and hugged her aunt. "Do you think if you called Uncle Harry he could get here before Clark comes? I don't see what it can hurt if he gives Dad a blessing. There's no reason Mom ever needs to know."

Chapter 10
Jean and Mae

(August 1971)

When Jean rolled over, the harsh noontime sun slapped her full in the face. She turned to the wall and tried to slide back into sleep, but the glaring light combined with the pervasive aroma of frying bacon and percolating coffee pulled her toward wakefulness. She lay for a moment, taking in the stillness and the superheated air, then pulled on a t-shirt and a pair of shorts and walked into the kitchen.

Mae, stylishly attired in a smart lime green linen dress with navy trim, her champagne blonde hair pulled back into a French Roll, stood at the stove frying bacon. Two beefsteak tomatoes waited on the counter. She turned when she heard Jean and rushed to embrace her, still clutching the spatula in one hand. They held one another tightly until Mae pulled away.

"I thought you were going to sleep all day. I'm fixing us BLTs – yum!"

"But how did you get here? You weren't even leaving until today. Did you drive all night?" While she talked she tied an apron around Mae's waist.

Mae smiled, her pale blue eyes twinkling. "Flew. First

time in my life! That's why I'm so dressed up." She pirouetted and raised her eyebrows questioningly. "Is this a great outfit or what? I've got some matching pumps somewhere around here." She looked under the table and around the other side of the stove. "Oh, there they are! Anyway, I called my boss last night and told him what happened and he said to take as much time as I needed. I got a 5:00 a.m. flight to Boise and Will arranged a free loaner car for me with his boss. I got here just in time to pick some tomatoes and make you lunch. Surprised?"

Jean tried to speak but her throat closed and her eyes filled. Mae set down the spatula and held her younger sister and let her cry until the kitchen began to fill with smoke.

"Oh damn!" Mae carried the pan out the door, smoke trailing behind her, and dumped the charred bacon on a bare patch of earth next to the flowerbed. She left Shep sniffing and biting at the hot bacon as it cooled.

Jean held the screen door for her as she came back in and began to cut more bacon from the slab. "You do look fabulous! What do you weigh – all of a hundred pounds?" They chitchatted while the bacon fried, avoiding the elephant in the room, until they were sitting at the table with their BLTs. Mae poured herself another cup of black coffee, but Jean demurred and grabbed a coke instead.

"I usually want my coffee first thing in the morning, but, Geez Louise, it's already noon and must be ninety degrees out," Jean said, smothering her tomato with salt before handing the shaker to Mae. Jean savored the crisp smoked meat, the crunchy garden lettuce, the firm juicy tomato. "Perfect. Is there anything that screams summer like a bacon, lettuce, and tomato sandwich?" She paused. "Have you talked to Mom yet?"

Mae held up a finger to signal her mouth was full, then swallowed and wiped juice from her hands. "No, she must be over at the hospital. The Chevy was gone when I got here.

The only thing out there is Dad's junky old pickup. I figured we'd head over to Ontario once you woke up so she can stop worrying about me and put her mind at ease, about me anyway." Her voice caught slightly. "How is Dad? Is there any change?"

As they finished their sandwiches, Jean filled her in, describing in detail Clete's swollen face, the tubes, the monitors. "You won't recognize him, Mae. It's horrible. I guess I always thought he was too mean to die, but now seeing him lying there. . . It's so confusing. I can't figure out *what* I feel. I keep crying and I don't even know what I'm crying about. Do you know what I mean?"

Mae sipped her steaming bitter coffee and stared out the window. "Yeah, I think I do. I've spent the last several years trying to avoid thinking about him. That's why I haven't been home for three years – not since that Christmas when he and Mom got in that screaming match on Christmas Eve. Remember that? If I'd had a car I would have left right then – and taken you with me. I made a promise to myself that I'd never put myself through that again, and I haven't. If that's what love and marriage is like, I want no part of it. I get all the love I need from Mr. Hyde, thank you."

Mae reached over and squeezed Jean's hand. "I sure love you, though."

Jean squeezed her hand back. "Good old Mr. Hyde. Bit of an attitude though. Is he still getting into it with the neighbor's Siamese?"

"Oh, yeah, and every other cat in the neighborhood."

"Have you ever considered that he might be the tabby version of Dad? What would Freud say about that?"

"Oh God!" Mae rolled her eyes. "Actually, though, he might be more like Mom. He weighs nearly twenty pounds now and he's sassy. Thank God he doesn't drink." Mae's voice took on a bitter edge. "And how is Mom? Is she still doing the Bette Davis routine?"

Jean picked at bits of fallen bacon before answering. "You know, Mae. I'm not so sure it is an act. Cass says she wants to talk to the two of us about Mom when this is all over and I get the feeling she has something important to tell us. And I had a long talk with Aunt Opal, who, by the way, has a lot more going on than I ever realized. I've got so much to tell you that I don't even know where to . . ."

Two short rings interrupted her sentence. She picked up the phone and listened for a moment, her brow furrowing.

"Mae is here too. She took a plane to Boise and drove over in one of Will's rental cars. We'll get there as fast as we can."

She put down the receiver and looked at Mae. "That was Clark. The doctor said we need to get there as soon as we can. Dad's going downhill fast. Can you clean up while I comb my hair and throw on some make-up? I'll tell you about my conversations with Aunt Opal and Cass on the way."

* * * * *

When Mae and Jean walked into the waiting room, Cass was sitting in a chair flipping through a copy of *Redbook Magazine*. She looked up when she heard them enter.

"Mae? Lordy, how did you get here so fast?" She grabbed Mae and enveloped her in a fleshy embrace. In Cass's arms, Mae looked like a child.

"Flew," she muttered, nestling her head deeper into Cass's bosom. "I've missed you Cass."

"The feeling is mutual." She held Mae out away from her and looked her up and down. "Are you getting littler with the years or am I getting bigger?"

Mae smiled. "I refuse to answer that." She hugged Cass again. "Have you heard anything?"

"Not a word since Clark called you," Cass replied. "You'll need to have the nurse buzz you in. Your mom and Clark are in there now."

Moments later they were engaged in a losing battle with the nurse at the desk, who was strictly enforcing the "two family members at a time" rule, when Dr. Rayburn walked through the door wearing green surgical scrubs, a mask dangling from his neck.

"Is there a problem?" he asked. Jean explained that they were trying to get in to join the rest of their family. Dr. Rayburn, after clearing the way for them with the disapproving nurse, turned to Mae with his hand extended.

"I'm Walt Rayburn. You are. . ."

"Mae. Mae Algood." Mae shook his hand and smiled, that familiar dazzling smile that had bewitched the boys in high school while simultaneously keeping them at a distance. Jean thought she could almost see the doctor's knees buckle.

Dr. Rayburn ran his hand through his hair, looked down and cleared his throat. "I'll take you in. I was on my way to talk to your mother anyway. He seems to be stabilizing again, for the time being anyway. He's a tough old bird, your dad."

As Dr. Rayburn held the door open for the girls to pass through, they were greeted by the metronomic cadence of the machines. Oleta was sitting in a chair pulled next to Clete's head and Clark was standing beside her. Jean was shocked by the radical change in both of them. Clark's eyes were bloodshot, the skin beneath them dark and puffy. His hair was a mess, his shirt wrinkled. Oleta, on the other hand, evinced none of the hysteria of the previous day and had donned a red sleeveless sheath dress. She looked ready to go out for a nice dinner.

When she saw Mae her composure momentarily crumpled. She jumped up and hugged her hard, choking back a sob and resting her cheek on the top of Mae's head.

Dr. Rayburn checked Clete's chart while the family greeted one another, then asked them to step out of the room for a moment so they could talk.

"Why can't we talk right here where we are? Mae hasn't

even had a chance to see her dad yet, for God's sake!" Jean was stunned by the disdain and rudeness in her mother's voice. But mostly she was surprised by the simmering rage.

Dr. Rayburn showed not the slightest irritation, instead he reached out and touched Oleta's arm lightly. "Of course, Mrs. Algood, it was thoughtless of me. I'll check on some of the other patients I need to see and come back in half an hour or so." He returned Clete's chart to the end of the bed, nodded to the three siblings, and left.

"I've got a tube of lipstick older than him," Oleta muttered. Jean opened her mouth to defend him, but gave it up. She did notice that Mae had followed him with her eyes until the door had closed.

When Dr. Rayburn returned he explained Clete's condition. He was gentle and compassionate, but could not have been more clear or less hopeful. He told them that Clete could not possibly survive more than a few days, probably less. Besides his catastrophic injuries, his kidneys were shutting down, he had increased brain swelling, and had developed pneumonia. Miraculously his heart rate was still steady, but that would change.

"I know how hard this is. I lost my parents in an automobile accident a few years ago and my mom lingered, hooked up to machines, for weeks before I lost her. Sometimes when there is no hope it's best to let nature take its course."

Oleta looked at him as if he were a viper. "What the hell are you saying? That we give up? Let him die? What kind of doctor are you?"

Before anyone else could react, Mae took her mother by the shoulders, and looked her squarely in the face. "Mom, listen to the doctor. Dad is suffering and we're prolonging it. Just look at him!"

Oleta looked from Mae to Clark to Jean, then rested her hand on Clete's arm. Silence enveloped the room, punctuated only by the steady beep, beep, beep. It seemed to Jean that, as she watched, her mother began to shrink, as though the fury draining out of her was the only thing sustaining her. Clark put his arm around her for support and she nodded her head in assent.

Three hours later they were all back in the waiting room sitting in the uncomfortable chairs and staring at the sickly green walls. Against all odds, when the breathing tube had been removed, Clete had continued breathing on his own. They had finally decided to take a break and return to shifts, someone constantly at his side. Cass, still parked in the waiting room, had been joined by Opal. Cass convinced Oleta to go to the Elks Lodge with her for a quick drink and Clark crashed on one of the couches within minutes of leaving the ICU.

The afternoon crawled on. Clark stretched and awoke after a three-hour nap. Betty and Leroy stopped by with a basket of fried chicken and potato salad. They talked, they ate, they waited.

Shortly before six Mae walked out of the ICU to be relieved by Clark. She sat on the arm of Oleta's chair. "He's still the same. Do you mind if Jean and I make a quick trip home so I can change? I've been in this outfit since five a.m. Do you want us to get you a change of clothes?"

Oleta, who was playing a game of three-handed cribbage with Cass and Opal, patted her on the knee. "Thanks, Sugar. I'm doing ok. A couple of whiskey sours and a hand of cards are perking me right up. You and Jean go on now, but don't be gone too long."

Mae raced the seventeen miles to Vale, slowed long enough to get through town, then floored it the last five miles, pulling into the farmyard in a billow of loose dust. She quickly changed into a white blouse and jeans. Forty minutes after leaving Ontario the two girls were in the car and on their way back.

Mae braked as they entered the Vale city limits, windows down, their hair whipping in the breeze, throwing Jean forward.

"You drive like a bat out of hell, you know that?"

Mae grinned.

As they passed Hawk's Tavern, Mae pulled up to the curb and turned off the car. "Mom's not the only one who could use a drink. We can be back in the car in fifteen minutes. What do you think?"

Jean eyed the familiar red door and thought for a minute. "I haven't been in there since I was a kid waiting for Dad and Mom. Sure. I guess it's fitting."

It took a few minutes for their eyes to transition from the intense late afternoon sun to the smoky dimness of the tavern. Tammy Wynette crooned over the click of one pool ball striking another. Other than the pool players and an old man staring into his drink at the end of the bar, they were the only patrons in the tavern. They chose the two stools nearest the door. Jean studied the stained glass surrounding the bar mirror and let her eyes drift to the jukebox and the pool table. "Last time I was here we were drinking Shirley Temples, reading comic books, and waiting for Mom and Dad to take us home."

"Well aren't you two all growed up and looking fine! What can I get for you beautiful young ladies? Are you still partial to Shirley Temples?" Earl Hawk, his black hair turned battleship grey, emerged from a back room and stepped behind the counter.

Mae tucked a loose strand of hair behind her ear. "Well, hell, Earl, I think I'll get something a bit stronger. How about a Tom Collins?" They both laughed and Jean ordered a rum and coke, weak. They asked about Earl's older sons, whom they had known in high school, and Jean told him she had seen Robbie working at the Dairy Queen.

Earl set the drinks on the bar. "So how's your dad doing?

I heard he was hurt pretty bad."

Jean took a swallow of her drink and grimaced, regretting not getting a plain coke. "We're on our way back to the hospital, have to leave in a few minutes actually. The doctor isn't too hopeful."

"You be sure to tell Oleta that I'm thinking of her."

Earl rested his forearms on the bar and leaned forward. "I wish you could have known your dad when we was young. He was something else. He was always laughing, telling a joke, singing some goddamned song." He smiled wistfully.

Mae downed the last of her drink in one swallow. "Yeah, would've been nice." She set her empty glass on the bar. "We'd best be getting back. It was good to see you Earl." She reached in her purse for her wallet, but Earl stopped her.

"On the house. You remember to give my best to Oleta, now." Jean left her drink sitting on the bar, largely untouched. As they opened the door to step outside they were blasted by a wall of heat and blinded by the glaring light.

"God," Mae said as she squinted to see. "I need to get some sunglasses tomorrow or my eyes are going to blister."

As they pulled away from the tavern, Jean looked over towards Mae, who drove with one arm resting on the window, looking relaxed and carefree.

"I can't believe you called him Earl. You sounded like a regular or something."

"What am I supposed to call him? Mr. Hawk? We're not kids now, Jean."

As they passed the community swimming pool and rounded the curve, Mae floored it to pass a slower car. Jean braced herself to keep from sliding into the door.

"No, we're not kids, but I sure feel like one around here. You know what Earl said about Dad? What he was like when he was young? I don't know, Mae. I'm not sure I would have liked him, even then. He sounds like one of those cock-sure jocks I can't stand."

"Yeah, maybe. Or maybe he was flat-out fun and having a shot-gun wedding and a passel of kids sucked all the joy out of him."

"Could be, but I think there's more to it than that. Something about the way Cass acted. I can't wait to talk to her."

Vale Butte loomed in the distance. On their left lustrous green hops draped over acres of supports, on the right fields of sugar beets stretched to the horizon. They drove in silence for a few miles, lost in their thoughts.

Jean wriggled out of her sandals and put her bare feet on the dashboard. "When I talked to you last month you were dating that grad student at PSU. How's that going?"

"Oh, he's past history. Once I realized I preferred to read a book than go out with him, I figured it was time to cut him loose."

"Geez, Mae. You could start a Boyfriend of the Month Club. Every time I talk to you you've moved on to a new one."

Mae signaled a left turn into the hospital parking lot. "You're one to talk. You just stretch it longer – Boyfriend of the Quarter, or something. Besides, I figure it's a damn sight better to spend my life with Mr. Hyde than end up trapped like our parents."

"There's got to be another option, don't you think? Say, what do you think of Dr. Rayburn? You made quite an impression on him."

"Dr. Rayburn? Seriously?"

"I'm telling you, you turned his head."

"He does have a cute nose – all those freckles marching across the bridge."

Mae pulled into a parking space and turned off the car. The two girls sat for a moment. "It felt good to talk about something besides Dad."

Cass was waiting for them as they walked into the waiting room. "Hurry on back, girls. Your father just passed."

Chapter 11
The Wake

"I'd think twice about eating those scalloped potatoes if I were you," Will whispered in her ear.

Jean paused, the serving spoon dangling in midair, and raised her eyebrows in a silent question.

"Some lady from the church made them," he hissed. "They've got enough fat in them to clog every artery in your body, if you can keep them down, which is doubtful. At something like this, I make it a practice to avoid anything baked in a casserole dish or anything that jiggles. The best bet is whatever is cooling in the tub on the porch and provided by Earl Hawk."

"That's something I'd like to see – you drinking a cold beer in front of your mother."

"True. But the operative phrase there is *in front of*. With all the people coming and going today, I can help myself to one or two on the sly and she'll be none the wiser."

Jean shook her head. "Twenty-two years old and still sneaking around your mother. Pitiful. Besides, Aunt Opal would smell alcohol on your breath from three houses over, and you know it." She surveyed the table. "Can you believe this spread?"

Cass's over-sized dining room table was covered from end

to end with fried chicken, Swedish meatballs, quivering Jell-O salads in an array of colors, two enormous hams, baskets of rolls, sliced tomatoes, green salads, macaroni salads, potato salads, butter pickles, sweet pickles, dill pickles, and an astonishing assortment of casseroles. In the center of it all was a pungent arrangement of lilies brought from the funeral. Three folding tables crowded against the wall were overflowing with desserts – apple pies, cherry pies, rhubarb pies, berry pies, a four-layer red velvet cake, carrot cakes, angel food cakes, and one enormous jellyroll coated in powdered sugar. Behind the desserts a rotating fan with an uneven blade ruffled the hot dry air with a fwap, fwap, fwap. Muted talking spilled from the kitchen, where half a dozen women worked to keep the food supplied and the dishes washed. Jean recognized the voices of Betty Fulmer and Mariko Matsui, the mother of a classmate, but was not entirely certain who the other voices belonged to.

Her mother's loud husky laugh echoed from the back porch where she was holding court with Cass. The increase in decibel level over the past two hours told her that Oleta was at least two sheets to the wind and working on a third. Jean quickly filled two plates. She found the cloying scent of the lilies oppressive.

"I'd better get this plate out to Mom before she embarrasses the entire family. Being in the limelight doesn't bring out the best in her – even at a time like this."

Will put one arm around her shoulders and squeezed. "Don't worry about it. When you're the grieving widow you get a pass." Jean leaned her head quietly against Will's shoulder for a brief moment as he held the door open for her. He followed her out to the broad wrap-around porch. Oleta, her eyes shining, lounged in a wicker chair surrounded by a crowd of friends and neighbors. Cass, fanning herself with an old paper fan and looking flushed and wilted, sprawled on the matching divan. Earl Hawk, beer in hand, had pulled a chair between Oleta and Lloyd Hillman, a hunting buddy of Clete's who had driven all the way from Portland for the funeral. Leroy Fulmer sat quietly next to Cass.

"So I've got this enormous buck in my sights – hell, must have been six, seven points, and I'm about to squeeze the trigger when Clete trips and down he goes – made enough noise to wake the dead – and the buck takes off. I wanted to strangle the son of a bitch. He's lucky he survived this long after that shenanigan. Jesus H. Christ!"

Oleta laughed, a little too loudly. "Hell, Lloyd, that probably wasn't no accident – he just didn't want you to have bragging rights for bagging that big buck."

Oleta looked up as the screen door banged shut and spotted Jean. "Oh, hey, here's my girl, bringing me a plate. Come sit down here with me for a minute, honey. I don't know where Mae and Clark has got off to."

Jean handed the plate to Oleta as Earl stood to offer her his seat. He perched on the edge of the wicker footstool. Will stood behind Jean, leaning against the porch railing.

Two large fans were aimed at the group from both sides of the porch, one of them blowing over the large tub of ice and beer. Jean noted that Aunt Opal was sitting directly in front of the tub sipping from a bottle of diet 7-Up, talking to Doris Oxman and Virgie Condon.

Jean leaned her head back and whispered to Will. "The cat's guarding the henhouse. You'd better come up with plan B."

Will whispered back. "Not to worry, I'll put Earl on it when he gets up."

"Put me on what, Will?" Earl asked. Will signaled with his eyes toward his mother sitting behind and to the right of him and pantomimed drinking a beer.

"Ah, got it." Earl turned back to Oleta. "Remember that Legionnaire's convention over to Timberline Lodge up there outside of Portland? Must have been what, '56, '57? Lloyd, you were there, weren't you?"

"Hell yes! I never missed one. That's where I met Clete and Oleta – at a Legionnaire's convention in Salem, I think it was. We got to talking over a bottle of Seagram's Seven and the next thing I know we're planning a hunting trip. I came out that same fall and haven't missed but one year since."

"That one up at Timberline was a humdinger. That was back before Eunice up and decided she'd had enough of me. We had the room next to Oleta and Clete. Remember that, Oleta?'

"Hells bells, how could I forget? You and Clete got so damned drunk that the people across the hall complained to the front desk because you was singing so loud. About three o'clock me and Eunice went to bed in one room and left you two singing in the other. We wanted to shoot you both. How's Eunice doing these days, anyway?"

Earl chuckled. "She's living out Nampa way with that fella she married. He got big as a barn – I don't know how he even gets through the door. I guess she likes that better than my drinking though. Can't say as I blame her. Me and Clete neither one of us ever knew when to stop. We had us some high times though. Fishing with Leroy here, or out camping up in the Strawberry Mountains with Clark and my boys when they was little. He was a good man, Clete Algood. Bad drunk, but a good man, take him all and all."

Earl's statement was followed by a long pregnant pause during which no one spoke. Oleta picked at her potato salad, then set the plate aside. "Not enough mustard," she grumbled, half to herself, then picked up her beer and took another swallow.

"Mom, you need to eat. You haven't eaten all day."

Oleta shot Jean a withering look. "Are you my daughter or my mother? I've got enough fat reserves to last me for quite some time. I'm sure as hell not going to starve anytime soon."

Cass put a hand on Oleta's arm. "This time Jean is right, honey. You need to eat. As your best friend I am cutting you off until you get some food in you."

"Will, could you go get a big hunk of one of those rhubarb pies – and have the ladies in the kitchen put some ice cream on it. Oleta never met a pie she could resist."

Oleta leaned back and closed her eyes.

Leroy cleared his throat. "You know, that was a real nice service in that little stone chapel they turned into a mortuary."

Opal, who had ended her conversation and begun to listen in on the general one, walked over to the larger group and sat on the edge of the divan next to Cass. "It wasn't too bad, was it? Of course, I was hoping Oleta would let the Bishop conduct the service, but that was Oleta's call and the mortician did it up real nice. I do love hearing Marian Nielson sing *In the Garden* — it gives me the chills every time. You know, our Daddy, rest his soul, helped to build that little church back in the early thirties when they first moved to this valley."

Oleta fastened Opal with a steely look. Her speech was slurred. "We didn't need no damned Mormon Bishop or no Marian Nielson neither. What we needed was Clete's family. Where the hell was Cloris? What kind of person don't even come to her own twin brother's funeral? And nobody gives a rat's ass who built the goddamned chapel."

Opal's eyes welled with tears.

Jean reached out and squeezed Opal's hand. "Mom, that's not fair. Aunt Opal has been here for you every *minute* since Dad's accident and you know it."

Cass stopped fanning herself and looked directly at Opal. "I'm not completely sure because I haven't seen her in nearly twenty-five years, but I think Cloris *was* there – at the cemetery anyway."

"She was there? When? Where did you see her?" Opal was palpably agitated. Oleta's face drained of color.

"While everyone was standing around waiting for the grave to be dedicated, I noticed a tall woman standing next to a beige Volvo parked by that big old Cottonwood. She caught my eye because of the car. My dad always loved Volvos. When she saw me looking at her, she turned away, but I'm pretty sure it was her. She was tall and lean and she had that sandy hair like you and Clete, cut real short, like a man. At first I thought it was a man, but the more I think about it the surer I am it was Cloris all right. I turned away when Harry started saying the prayer and when I looked up again she was gone."

Oleta and Opal were both visibly shaken.

Will, slamming the screen behind him, handed Cass a messy piece of rhubarb pie drowning in melting ice cream. Opal daubed at her eyes with a tissue and blew her nose. Will rested a hand on her shoulder.

"Are you OK, Mom? Can I get you something?" He cast an inquiring glance.

Jean silently mouthed, "I'll tell you later."

Opal smiled at Will and stood up. "No thank you, honey. I think I'll go check on the kitchen crew and see how they're getting on. It sounds like they're starting to clean up now that most of the folks are heading home. I might even go lie down for a bit, if that's all right with you, Cass."

"Best idea you've had all day. Turn left at the top of the stairs and stretch out on the guest bed."

Oleta leaned back in the chair and closed her eyes. "I'm sorry, Opal. I'm not myself today."

"No apology necessary, you know that." She squeezed Oleta's hand. Oleta squeezed back.

Cass handed Oleta a tissue and coaxed her to eat the pie. After a minute or two had passed Oleta wiped her eyes and took the fork Cass was pushing on her and ate the pie and ice cream. Opal nearly collided with Clark as he pushed open the screen door, two heaping plates in his hands. He laughed when he saw the empty pie plate and the full dinner plate next to Oleta.

"Maybe I'd better go trade this in at the dessert table. I forgot how much you love pie!" Oleta lit up when she saw

Clark. Virgie and Ed Condon came by to pay their respects on their way out, the old librarian's calm presence easing the tension. Earl and Lloyd struck up a side conversation with Leroy. Cass sat up and rubbed her lower back.

"Lordy," Cass said, "I do believe that if I don't get up right now I may never rise again. I should not have had those two beers. In fact, I should never touch alcohol – can't handle it. Never could. Always makes me run off at the mouth. Jeannie, what do you say to a stroll to get the blood flowing? Where's Mae gone off to, anyway?"

"Last time I saw her she was under the big elm out front talking to Leroy's sons. I swear, she's a magnet to men, married or single, young or old."

Cass pulled herself heavily out of the chair, struggling to right herself. For the first time it struck Jean how much Cass was aging. Even though Cass was the same age as her mother, Cass had always seemed so vivacious and young in spirit that Jean had never really thought of her as middle-aged. She looked at her now with new eyes – the rolls of sagging flesh, the puffy eyes – and recognized that Cass was not a healthy woman.

She took a coke from the tub, popped the top, and held out her arm so Cass could steady herself on the steps. A few friends and neighbors were still gathered in small groups under the three large sycamores in the back yard, some sitting on folding chairs, others on the grass. Many were fanning themselves with the paper program from Clete's funeral.

The short service had been held at the mortuary mid-morning, after the milking but early enough to complete the burial before the stifling August heat built up. Throughout the service a handsome young Clete had grinned rakishly from a framed photograph resting on an easel, looking as though he were ready to step out of the frame and cause trouble. Lloyd had delivered the eulogy, two of Oleta's brothers had given prayers, and Marian Nielson, who sang at most of the funerals in town, had warbled her way through her signature song. The entire funeral was over in forty-five minutes. Everyone had followed the hearse out to the cemetery west of town for the burial then gone on to Cass's house after. Jean had been comforted by the stories and laughter, but now she was ready for everyone to go home.

*****

Cass and Jean found Mae sitting alone in the swing on the front porch petting Buttons, Cass's miniature Dachshund, who was curled beside her. Buttons thumped his tail when he heard Cass, but made no sign of moving.

Cass picked him up and dropped him on the ground, lowering herself tipsily into his place. The swing creaked from her weight. Jean perched on the porch rail leaning against a post. Several guests passed by them on their way out, giving their regards. The only sounds were quiet laughter and conversation from the back and soft panting from Buttons, who had found a cooler spot under the swing.

Cass pulled a cigarette pack from her pocket. "Jean, can you reach me that ashtray on the rail." She leaned back and closed her eyes, enjoying her cigarette. "God, I hate funerals. And why do they always have to be in August? Did you know my husband Archie died in August too? And, of course, Jimmy and Joey."

Jean watched the shimmering heat waves undulate across the pavement. In the weedy lot across the street, a battered Silver Stream rested on a stack of cinder blocks. The air was still, lifeless. Even the birds seemed to be waiting out the August heat.

"Cass, can you tell us more about what happened after the twins died? I think it might help us understand Dad and Mom a bit more. Up at the hospital Aunt Opal told me about how it happened and I told Mae about it. It must have been unimaginably horrible for Mom and Dad, but they never talked about it, or even about Jimmy and Joey. It was a forbidden subject."

Mae rested her hand lightly on Cass's leg. "Yes, Cass, please."

Chapter 12
Cass's Story Continues

Cass closed her eyes and leaned back. "When my Archie died I thought my world had ended. All around me was like a jubilee, everyone celebrating the end of the war and the men starting to come home. Everyone but Archie. I didn't think I would survive it, not after losing both my parents and my brother, but I did. Somehow I did. Archie was a grown man and a soldier, so his death was, well not exactly natural, but it was something I could come to accept. It took a long, long time, but every day it got a little easier. But those little boys! There isn't anything natural about two three-year-old boys drowning on their birthday and it's not something you ever get over. I thought it would kill Oleta. In fact, it nearly did.

"That first month or so after the boys died was a blur. I felt so much guilt. I should've been there that day – maybe one more pair of eyes would've made the difference. But the first anniversary of Archie's death had sucked me back down into a black void and I couldn't stand the thought of being around those little boys, knowing I would never have a family of my own." So I lied to Oleta, told her I had a stomach bug. Instead of being there where I should have been, I stayed at home wallowing in self-pity. Maybe it wouldn't have made any difference, but I'll always wonder.

"After the accident I took a week off to help her out, but then I had to go back to work. It was like I was watching myself from across the room. I worked at the Vale Grocery back then and I'd ring up folks' eggs and milk and what not, make a little small talk, but I wasn't really there, if you know what I mean. Those first few weeks I tried so hard to be some help to Oleta, but I'd go out there to try to comfort her and all I'd do was sit and cry. I was so low I wasn't much use at all. She didn't cry, though. That was the worst part. She would just sit there drinking black coffee with a hollow look in her eyes and fidget, like she couldn't wait for me to leave.

"It's not in my nature to be sad, can't seem to sustain it for too long. By the end of September I had pulled myself out of it and felt strong enough to be a real friend to your mom. I expected her to be like I was after Archie died – go through the worst of the grieving like a sleepwalker and then start to get a little stronger and more accepting with each day that passed. By early November, though, it was clear that she was sinking deeper and deeper into a black and bottomless place. It was like watching her drowning in quicksand while I stood by helpless. . . ."

(November 1946 – August 1947)

Blustery north winds buffeted the small Volvo sedan as Cass maneuvered the narrow road atop the embankment leading to Clete and Oleta's farm. The leafless cottonwoods at the end of the lane loomed over the shabby barn and even shabbier house enshrouded by dead and dying vegetation. Everything was as it had always been, but now a melancholy had wrapped itself like a pernicious vine around the fields and buildings. Clete's Chevy was parked in front of the house, but since Bob did not come to greet her Cass assumed the two of them were off in the fields somewhere. Several late pansies blooming amidst the dying foliage only heightened the dread of impending winter. The silent house seemed to watch her approach.

Clark was sitting alone at the kitchen table coloring a picture of a cat with a stubby red crayon. He looked up solemnly as Cass entered. "Do you have any crayons, Cass? These is almost all gone."

Cass kissed him on the head. "Sure, buddy. I'll bring some the next time I come out. Do you want the great big box?"

Clark's eyes widened. "Could I?"

"You bet you can, if you give your Auntie Cass some sugar."

Clark gave her a quick kiss and went back to his coloring.

"Those are great whiskers that cat's got." Cass studied the drawing from over Clark's shoulder. "Maybe we should see if your mom would let you come stay with me sometime soon. We could go the movies and play games, even get some ice cream at the Dairy Queen. Would you like that? I get real lonely in that big house all by myself."

Clark leveled her with a solemn gaze and shook his head. "I can't. Mommy needs me to help her so she won't be so sad."

"Where is your mom, Clark?"

"She's outside. She likes to go for walks. I go with her so she won't be lonely, but it got too cold so she said it'd be alright if I came in." Clark resumed his coloring, selecting an even stubbier blue crayon for the sky.

Cass looked around the kitchen. The counter and sink were piled high with dirty dishes. The half-empty milk pail sat on the counter. Cass put the milk in the icebox and tousled Clark's coarse brown hair. "I think I'll go find her and see if I can talk her into coming in."

She spotted Oleta at the back of the east pasture, on the edge of the alkaline waste that led to the river, a lonely figure etched against the empty sky, motionless in the rustling stubble field of late autumn. Cass cupped her hands and shouted

Oleta's name into the wind, wishing she had worn a heavier coat. Oleta turned and started back toward Cass.

Oleta's wind-whipped hair had not been combed and she wore no makeup. Only a lightweight jacket covered her cotton housedress. Her gloveless hands were raw and red, her legs bare. Her dress hung on her gaunt frame as though it had been made for a much larger woman. She neither smiled nor greeted Cass, but she did turn and walk back with her to the house.

Clark was standing at the door waiting to open it when they came in. He took his mother's hand and led her to the table to see his picture, climbing into her lap like a very small child. Oleta smiled wanly while resting her cheek wearily on Clark's head. Cass grabbed a quilt from the foot of the bed and wrapped it around Oleta before starting a pot of coffee. While the coffee percolated, Cass moved all the dirty dishes to the counter and filled the sink with soapy water.

"Where is Clete today? I see his car is still here."

Oleta looked out the window as if seeing the car for the first time. "I don't know."

Cass filled a large mug with black coffee and set it in front of her. Oleta didn't move.

"Drink that, it will warm you up." Cass pushed the mug closer to Oleta and began washing the dishes. "Will he be coming in for dinner? It's past noon."

Oleta held the warm mug in her hands and stared vacantly into space. "I don't know."

Cass tried again. "What shall I fix for you and Clark?" When Oleta didn't answer, Cass got down on her knees so she was eye-level with Clark. "Are you hungry, Clark?"

Clark looked at Cass out of haunted eyes and burrowed deeper into Oleta's bosom. "Uh-huh."

Cass found a shepherd's pie in the icebox with Opal's name written on the side of the pan. It looked fairly fresh, so she put it in the oven. She could find no bread.

"When was the last time you baked, Oleta?"

"I don't know."

Cass poured herself a cup of coffee, stirred in some milk and a teaspoon of sugar, and sat down at the table. "Clark, honey, how about you run off and play until dinner is ready so your mom and I can talk?"

Clark looked at his mother as if asking for permission. Oleta kissed him and told him to go ahead. Clark picked up his drawing and crayons and went into his bedroom.

"Oleta, what were you doing out there in the field? You could catch pneumonia and then what would Clark do?" She took a swallow of coffee, shuddered, and added another teaspoon of sugar.

Oleta clasped the mug in her hands and stared into the blackness. "I don't know. I just can't stand being in this house, Cass. It's like the walls are closing in on me. It's better now, with you here, but when I'm alone or it's only me and Clark . . ." She shuddered and rubbed her arms.

"Oleta, you've got to snap out of it. For Clark, if not your yourself."

Oleta sipped her coffee and said nothing. The silence was broken by Bob, who had seen Cass through the window and was barking excitedly as he ran towards the house. Cass stepped outside and knelt down to greet him as he bounded up the steps followed by Clete.

"I saw your car. Thought I'd come in and sit a spell."

Cass was startled. She could not remember a time when Clete had ever gone out of his way to speak to her – rather the opposite, in fact.

Cass filled a mug for Clete and they talked about the goings on in town, the weather, small talk. Oleta never looked up. When Cass called Clark to come have dinner and served up the casserole, Oleta picked at her plate listlessly. Cass had never enjoyed being around Clete. She hated the way he picked at Oleta and the constant bickering and tension. There was no arguing now, just a cavernous void that shouted more loudly.

After Clete returned to the fields, Cass stayed for the rest of the afternoon, long enough to bake bread and make a large pot of beef soup that would last them a few days. She left when Oleta lay down for a nap. Cass looked in on her before leaving and watched her for a moment before heading out into the fields to find Clete.

She turned the corner to cross the bridge over the drainage ditch and almost stumbled on him deep in conversation with Karl. Cass had not seen Karl for months, perhaps a year or more. He was so thin that his belt had been tied in a knot to hold his pants and his face was ghostly. He started when he saw her and immediately turned and strode across the fields toward the river.

"Wasn't that Karl Mueller? Is he sick?"

Clete dropped the butt of his cigarette and ground it out with his foot while speaking. "I don't know what to do about Oleta. I think she's not right in her head or something."

A gust of wind whistled through the ravine created by the deep ditch and both of them turned to face away from the biting wind. A line of tumbleweeds clung to the wire fence that separated Clete's pasture from the barren fields beyond. A hawk shrieked overhead.

Cass hugged herself, shivering from the cold. "I'm worried too. I'll talk to Opal and make sure someone comes out every couple of days to help out and check on her. We'll get her through it."

Clete continued to look down as he spoke, his voice shaking. "I figured maybe if she had another baby it would set things right. But, hell, she won't even let me touch her. They was my boys too." His voice broke, then he laughed ruefully, still grinding the butt with his toe. "It's too damn bad she wasn't like this when I met her. We'd both have been better off."

Cass flinched. Tentatively, she reached out a hand and

touched Clete on the arm. "She'll come around. You've got to give her time to work it out."

Clete nodded his head once, never looking up, and turned on his heel and walked off in the same direction Karl had gone.

For the rest of the winter Opal and Cass took care of Oleta and her household with the help of family and neighbors like the Fulmers, Oxmans and Condons. Cloris drove over from Boise at least every other Saturday. Even on bitter cold days Cass would often find Oleta walking the fields, sometimes with Clark bundled up against the cold, more often alone. Christmas was especially painful, but helping Oleta through it helped Cass through it. Holidays were still mine fields to Cass. By Easter Oleta was taking care of the household again, baking the bread, getting meals on the table, but she had dropped a frightening amount of weight and still wandered the fields, wraithlike, still responded in the same indifferent, lifeless tone. The only time she would become visibly agitated was when Cass or Opal tried to press her into making a trip into town for groceries or a movie or a visit to the Merc. She would not leave the farm. She refused to see anyone other than Cass or Opal or Betty and LeRoy Fulmer. When anyone else came, even her brothers and their wives, she would take to the fields or stay in her room.

Clete had retreated also, but in a different way. With Oleta he was always polite and solicitous, but no warmth flowed between them. He threw himself into the farm, improving the barn, building a new shed, repairing fences. When he was not working on the farm he spent whole days hunting pheasant or grouse and fishing the streams and lakes within a few hours' drive. Cass saw less and less of him as the long winter waned and spring fell into summer, even though she spent the better part of three days a week at the farm. With the warmer weather, Oleta spent even more time outside wandering the fields for hours at a time. Normally she kept the yard green and tidy with a large beautiful flowerbed. This year the only flowers were those that came up on their own, and even those struggled to survive. Inside the house beds remained unmade, dishes unwashed, floors unswept. Nevertheless, Cass never heard Clete say a word in complaint. Hours each day Oleta walked the far edges of the farm, Clark by her side. Never, however, would she cross the barbed wire barrier that separated their land from the alkaline fields to the east or the neighboring farms on either side. Cass tried everything to distract her, even teaching her to drive in her beloved Volvo. Oleta would never drive further than the end of the embankment, turning around at the cattle guard at the end of the road. By August Cass was convinced that Oleta's sanity might not survive the onslaught of another winter. . . .

****

"It was near the end of August, 1947, a little over a year after we lost Jimmy and Joey. I was sprawled out on my back porch spilling out of a pair of shorts and trying to beat the heat when I heard a car door slam and Oleta and Clark's voices. Mind you, Oleta had not left that farm for a year. God almighty, you've never seen a fat woman move as fast as I did that day. I was through the house and out the front door to meet them before they were halfway up the walk. She was standing there, smiling like she'd seen the second coming, and in her arms was a newborn baby. "I'm naming her Mae, after Mae West. Isn't she beautiful?"

(August 1971)

Mae and Jean looked at each other, dumbfounded.

"What?" Mae said. "You didn't say anything about her being pregnant. Funny, I always thought the twins died a couple of years before I was born. And didn't you say she wouldn't let Dad touch her? And that she was really thin? How is that possible?"

Cass had been talking almost as if to herself and was startled by Mae's rapid-fire questions. She struggled to get to her feet. "Damn that alcohol. I think I need to go for a walk and clear my head a bit."

Jean put out a hand to stop her. "Cass, sit down. You can't stop now. Did she hide the pregnancy from everyone and that's why she wouldn't go into town? But you'd think she would have been happy about that. It doesn't make sense."

Cass struggled to find a way out of the maze her loose tongue had led her into.

Mae's questions dangled in the air, but instead of answering she turned at the sound of the front gate being opened and pulled herself out of the swing to greet the tall thin woman walking purposefully towards them.

"Hello Cloris," Cass said.

"Cass."

"Girls, I'd like you to meet your Aunt Cloris."

Cloris was a tall woman with narrow hips, broad shoulders, and short wispy dishwater blonde hair. Her face, creased prematurely by age, lacked the handsome symmetry of Clete's face and the effect of the whole was not entirely pleasant. Her eyes, however, were stunning – seafoam blue freckled with bits of brown. Like Clete's eyes. It was not a beautiful face, or even an attractive one, but neither Jean nor Mae could take their eyes off of it.

Jean's tongue seemed tangled in knots and it was Mae who spoke first, holding out her hand. "I'm Mae and this is Jean. We've wanted to meet you for a long time."

Cloris's eyes filled with tears as she shook hands, first with Mae, then Jean. While she met the gaze of both girls, her eyes lingered longest on Mae. She reached in her pocket for a hankie and blew her nose. Clearing her throat, she turned to Cass.

"I didn't want to come until most people had gone on home." Her raspy smoker's voice dropped off at the end of each phrase and she still retained the slight western twang that characterized the speech of the people in the valley. "Hell, I don't even know what I'm doing here now."

Cass reached out and patted her reassuringly on the arm. "Oleta and Opal will be glad you've come. Oleta's out back on the porch. Opal's upstairs lying down. Will you be staying out on the farm with Opal and Harry?"

"I haven't thought that far yet. I just threw some things in the car in the middle of the night and started driving – didn't even know I was coming until then. I'll probably get a room at the Bates Motel. I like my morning coffee and Opal's not likely to appreciate me smoking in her house."

"You'll stay right here. I've got two empty bedrooms for God's sake. I make a mean cup of coffee and smoke like a chimney myself."

Cass led the way through the house. Most of the people had already left and all the perishable food had been removed from the table. Two pies and the collapsed remains of the jelly roll now shared the dining room table with the pickles, tomatoes, and a basket of rolls. The house echoed with the clinking of plates and the chatter of women working in the kitchen. Out back only a few close friends and neighbors remained. Lloyd and Earl bookended Oleta, who was slumped, exhausted, in her chair.

When the screen door slammed behind them Oleta looked up and the remaining color drained from her face. . . .

* * * * *

(A few hours later)

"One more year, you say? What are you going to do then?" Cloris fixed Jean with a gaze that bored into her.

"I don't know. Get a job somewhere bookkeeping I guess."

"That's what you want to do? Keep someone's books? Was that your idea or your father's?"

"Well, I *am* getting a degree in Accounting."

Cloris chuckled ruefully. "And I'm being pushy as hell, aren't I?"

"No, you're right. It was his idea. If I'd been a boy I would've been a vet.

But it's too late to change now, anyway."

"Don't do that to yourself. It's never too late – never. It's the 1970s, not the 1920s. You can do anything you set your mind to." Cloris drained her wine glass and poured herself another.

"What about you, Mae? Do you dream of keeping books too, or do you want to be a school teacher, like Clark?"

Mae smiled. "No, I leave higher education to my brother and sister. I put in my eight hours at the office then come home to Mr. Hyde and a good book. No fuss, no bother, no strings."

"Mr. Hyde?"

Jean interjected. "Mr. Hyde's her cat. Mae's the smartest one in the family too. I've been trying to get her to go to college for years."

Mae shrugged her shoulders. "I don't know why I should. If I want to know something I get books and learn it on my own. And my boss doesn't seem to care – last week he offered me a management position, which I'm thinking of turning down, by the way. Too much commitment. Who needs it?"

Cloris opened her mouth to speak, then closed it. Instead she picked up the wine bottle and studied the label. "Inglenook Cabernet Sauvignon – I was surprised to find this. I didn't think anyone in Vale knew a good wine from a bad one."

She tilted the bottle towards Cass's nearly empty glass. "More?"

Cass covered her glass with her hand. "No thanks."

"How about you, Mae?"

"No. One is enough for me. I'm not much of a wine drinker – gives me a headache."

Cloris poured the remainder of the bottle into her own glass. Holding the stem in her hand she swirled the contents, then raised her glass in a toast.

"To my new nieces, or at least new to me." Cloris drank half and set her glass down.

"I'd better eat something. I think I'm a little tipsy." She pushed away from the table, took a plate and fork out of the rack of dishes draining on the counter, and cut herself a piece of apple pie.

By the time Opal and Will finally left, around six, Oleta's nerves were stretched so taut that she had begun snapping at everyone, even Cass. Clark had taken her home, along with enough leftovers to fill every available space in the fridge. The remainder of the food had been left with Cass. She, Cloris, Mae and Jean had been sitting at the table talking for over two hours.

Cloris sat back down with her pie and took a bite. "This is delicious. It has to be Opal's." She stretched out with a satisfied look, patted her stomach, and lit another cigarette. Her eyes rested on Mae, who had risen to open the back door for Buttons.

"God, you look like your mother."

Mae turned, looking confused. "Like my mother? I'm the only one in the family who doesn't look like our mother. You mean like my dad?"

Cloris turned to Cass. "She doesn't know?"

Mae looked from one to the other. "Doesn't know what?"

Cass cleared her throat. "Damn. Mae, I think you'd better sit down. There's something I need to tell you."

Mae sat down and looked from Cass to Cloris and back again. "Tell me what, Cass?"

"Before Cloris came you asked me how your mom could have been pregnant. Well, she wasn't. When Oleta came out to the house that day holding you in her arms, it was like a miracle had occurred. I hadn't seen her really smile for a year, and there she was beaming from ear to ear. She told me that Doc Nelson knew a teenage girl from Nyssa that had gotten herself knocked up and needed a home for the baby. He'd told Clete about it, and Clete had brought her home. As far as Oleta was concerned, though, you were her own. From that day on she told everyone that you were hers, even made up details about your birth. Who was going to challenge her? Only a few of us knew the truth and most people hadn't even seen her for a year. You saved her, Mae. The old Oleta came back when you came into her life. She stopped wandering the fields, started going out, even started driving herself into town. At some point she started to believe her own fiction. I'm pretty sure she thinks she gave birth to you."

Jean knelt by Mae's chair and clasped her hands, looking up at her anxiously. Mae trembled and her voice shook.

"But I don't understand. I've got a copy of my birth certificate. My parents are recorded as Clete and Oleta Algood. How is that possible?"

"I don't know how it happened. Clete must have arranged it somehow. And remember, Mae, your mother truly believes you are her flesh and blood daughter."

"That explains Mom, but what about Dad? He sure as hell knew." She looked at Cloris. "You said I looked like my mother. Did you know my mother? Who is she? Do I know her?"

"No, you don't know her." Cloris's voice caught. "You've never met your mother because she died the day you were born."

Cass reached out and took both of Mae's hands. "Annie Mueller. Your mother's name was Annie Mueller. Jean, you have a picture of her. Remember that photo you showed me last week at lunch?"

Mae looked dazed. "What picture? What are you talking about?"

Jean rummaged in her purse and pulled the photo from a side pocket. "This picture. I meant to tell you about it, but with Dad's accident and everything I forgot. The old hermit down by the river died and Will and I went down to his cabin on a lark to rummage around, you know, like when we were kids. I found a picture of Dad in a coffee can. I showed it to Cass the morning that he had his accident."

Mae held the picture while the others gathered around her. "She was lovely. I do sort of look like her a bit, don't I? That's you, isn't it Cloris? Who is this boy next to her?"

Cass tapped the picture with a polished nail. "That is her brother Karl, the one you all call the hermit."

"Oh wow. I can't wait to tell Will," Jean said.

Mae was still studying the photograph. "But she would have been Dad's age, not a teenager when I was born. She was your friend, Cloris?"

Cloris blew her nose and cleared her throat. "She was the best thing in my life from the time I was in first grade. She was the gentlest, most beautiful human being ever to walk this earth. Everyone loved Annie, but nobody loved her like I did."

"Then you probably know who my father is too. Do you?"

Cass and Cloris looked at one another silently. Finally, Cloris spoke. "She deserves to know, Cass."

Cass reached over and put her hand on Mae's. "Clete is your father, Mae."

Jean and Mae both looked stunned.

"But how, I mean, there must be. . ."

Cloris drained her wine glass. "I'll tell you what I know, but I don't know all of it. It started a long time ago, back when we were in high school."

Chapter 13
Cloris and Annie:
Forms of Love

"I loved Annie more than I've ever loved anyone, but it was Clete who was the great love of her life. God knows why. She fell for him at the county fair right before our senior year in high school. Up to that time Clete and I were as close as a brother and sister could be, joined at the hip as they say. Annie was my best friend and her brother Karl was Clete's best friend. From the time we were snot-nosed kids in elementary school the four of us had been like this." Cloris crossed her fingers and held them up. "Karl was bullied because he was so shy and odd, so Clete became his protector at school, just like Annie tried to protect him from his sadistic father at home. We were together so much our other friends called us the four musketeers.

"But one day he turned that damned charm of his on Annie and my world changed. From then on, everything revolved around the two of them and Karl and I were left to hover around the fringes, like wannabes around the in-crowd. I might have handled it better if he'd been good to her, but he ran hot and cold. Strung her along, then broke it off; chased

131

after everything in skirts, then came back and she forgave everything. Hot and cold, on and off. It like to killed me, but through it all she never once gave up on him; never blamed him or accused him. I guess I did enough of that for both of us.

"After graduation she and I got an apartment together in Boise. It was a tiny little one-bedroom basement apartment under an old house, dark and depressing in the winter but cool in the summer. There were so many bugs in that place that we used to sweep up the dead ones every morning before breakfast. It had a lumpy double bed and a ratty old couch and we ate on the floor until we could find a kitchen table and a couple of chairs. Once we started making some money, Annie made a couch cover and a bedspread and some matching curtains to go with it. After the farms we had grown up on we thought we were living the high life. I went to work for the bank and she had a secretarial job. Clete would drive over every month or so, but every time he came it only made her unhappy. I got to where I started to hate him – my own brother. I didn't trust him and I guess I was jealous too. And then something happened sometime in the second winter, and you could feel the electricity between them. I had never really believed that he loved her before that, but by spring he was coming over nearly every weekend and they were talking marriage. He was always bringing her little trinkets and boxes of candy, writing her long mushy letters every few days. She wore a locket around her neck that he had given her with both their pictures in it. When Annie was happy she lit up a room, and when she was happy, I was happy. I even started to trust him again.

"Well, when August rolled around the visits slowed down and then the letters slowed down – practically stopped for a few weeks even – and Annie started to get worried. She wouldn't say anything against him, but I knew Annie so well that she couldn't hide it from me. He kept giving excuses why he couldn't get away to visit. When he finally did come over for Labor Day weekend she went away with him for a couple of days – she'd never done that before – and when she came back she was glowing and they were talking about a wedding in the spring. Five weeks later he told her he was marrying Oleta."

*****

(Early October, 1940)

The Saturday Clete was due to arrive was one of those glorious Indian summer days that make old folks reminisce. The sinuous curves of the Boise River snaking through town were lined with brilliant yellow willows and mottled brown underbrush. Red maples and golden poplars shimmered in a mild breeze. Dry leaves skittered across the road and into the front yard. Only the incessant barking of a dog in the distance punctured the morning stillness.

Cloris shaded her eyes as she stared down the dirt lane toward the paved street, then sat down on the top step of the basement stairs and lit another cigarette, her second since coming outside to wait. She inhaled deeply and practiced expelling the smoke in measured puffs while listening to the sounds from the river. After several minutes had passed she stood and stared down the street again, then resumed pacing back and forth. Her pole and tackle box leaned against the side of the house next to the coffee can full of night crawlers.

Every weekend since Labor Day Clete had made the two-hour drive from the ranch where he was working in Jordan Valley, arriving mid-morning on Saturday and leaving Sunday night. Cloris made plans each Saturday to be away from the house all day so Annie and Clete could be in the apartment alone, coming back in the early evening when they left to go out. Clete had always slept on the couch when he came, but now Cloris took the couch and left the bedroom to them.

Cloris dreaded the empty loneliness of those weekends and her stomach twisted into knots when she let herself think about a future without Annie beside her. The sight of Clete's battered black Ford brought with it a wave of jealousy and sadness.

On this second weekend in early October Cloris had planned a last fishing trip of the season with Ed and Marshall, two young men from work. She had talked them into going all the way up to the South Fork of the Boise River near Paradise by regaling them with tales of the huge cutthroat she had pulled out of that stretch of the river the previous autumn. She had wanted to leave at dawn, but Marshall had a date the night before and refused to get up before eight o'clock on a Saturday morning, saying he had had enough of that on the farm. Now, it was nearly nine and Cloris was getting increasingly agitated. The last thing she wanted was to be in the house to watch Annie's face light up when she saw Clete.

She heard the engine before she saw the car, relieved that it was Marshall's black Dodge sedan and not Clete's Ford. She stomped out her cigarette and was waiting with her gear before the car even came to a stop. She threw her things in the trunk and jumped in the back.

"What took you so damned long?" Cloris asked as she slammed the door.

Marshall rested his arm on the seat and craned his neck to look at her. "Christ-almighty, Cloris. Relax, will you. It's Saturday." Ed said nothing. The car did not move.

Cloris bit her tongue. "Alright. Sorry. I'm just champing at the bit to sink my hook into a cutthroat." The car still did not move. "Come on, let's go. I said I was sorry."

Marshall turned back around, made an excruciatingly slow U-turn in the road, and drove toward the street. They passed Clete on their way to the main road.

Under her breath, Cloris muttered to herself, "asshole," and lit another cigarette.

The drive up into the forest took several hours, but the

autumn colors and the dazzling blue of the early October sky eventually dissipated her black mood. Long before they reached the South Fork, Marshall and Cloris were trading good-natured insults, and Ed was chuckling along with them. They spent the afternoon hiking along the river, fishing some of Cloris's favorite holes. Ed had brought butter and spam sandwiches, which they ate while dangling their feet in the cool water. The temperatures in Boise had hovered in the low-seventies for the better part of a week and the forest, though cooler, was near perfect. Wandering apart from the others amidst the towering Ponderosas and narrow Lodge Pole Pines, Cloris found momentary respite from the inner turmoil that had rocked her for months.

It was nearing seven when Marshall pulled up in front of the brown clapboard house and Cloris jumped out. Clete's car was gone so she assumed they had gone out. The door slammed behind her and she squeezed past the table into the tiny corner kitchen and laid her catch on the counter. One twelve-inch cutthroat and a slightly smaller rainbow. She had slit the belly of the first and was sliding her thumb down the inside of the spine to snag the guts when she saw Annie's purse sitting on the couch. She paused for a moment, thinking only that Annie would be upset when she realized she had left it, and finished scaling and gutting both fish. Their big yellow tom rubbed against her legs and called plaintively until Cloris opened the screen and tossed the heads under the bushes for him. She didn't see Annie until she went into the bedroom to change into clean clothes.

Annie was curled up on the bed, her legs pulled up tightly against her chest, her eyes closed.

"Annie, what's wrong? Where's Clete?"

Annie did not move. When Cloris failed to get a response, she grabbed her by the shoulders and sat her up, attempting to look directly into her eyes. Annie looked away.

Cloris shook her gently. "Annie, talk to me."

Annie began to shake. She wrapped her arms around herself tightly and rocked back and forth. Cloris held her as she
cried and rocked.

When she finally could speak it was one word. "Oleta."

"Oleta? Oleta Lambson? What about Oleta?"

Annie stammered out the words. "He's marrying her. Oh,
God. She's pregnant, Cloris. He got her pregnant."

For the next week Cloris tended Annie as one would a sick
child. She took emergency leave to care for her and told
Annie's boss she had the flu. When Annie couldn't find the
strength to chew, Cloris made her soups and milkshakes that
were easier to get down. She sat with her through long sleepless nights, washed and brushed her hair, told jokes to try to
make her laugh. By the following Monday, a week and a half
later, Annie was strong enough to return to work, although
thin and pale. For most of the fall she came home from work
and crawled into bed. Cloris would hold her most of the night
as she cried herself out. She got so thin that Cloris worried
constantly about her. The only thing that brought Annie out
of herself was worry about her brother Karl. Clete's marriage
had left Karl alone on the ranch.

Every weekend for the next two months Cloris drove Annie to Jordan Valley to see him. When with Karl, Annie forced
herself to act cheerful. Annie pushed him to get a job closer to
Boise so he would be around other people, but Karl wouldn't
consider it. He had been hired by a Basque rancher with an
enormous spread and appeared to be more contented than he
had in years. The solitary days and hard work suited him.
The gaunt haunted look that had worried Annie so much disappeared, replaced by a healthy leanness. For the first time
in years, Cloris felt comfortable with him. The three of them
spent hours fishing the Owyhee River and Dry Creek or hiking
in the surrounding hills. In mid-November they took advantage of the unusually long Indian summer for a late camping trip in Leslie Gulch. The balmy temperatures of the day

dropped rapidly as clouds rolled in overnight and they broke camp at first light in a heavy snowfall, pelting each other with snowballs as they loaded Karl's pickup. To Cloris, Karl seemed more confident in the absence of Clete. On their outings he assumed the protective role Clete had always taken with the two girls. None of them spoke Clete's name or alluded to his absence. It was a wound far too fresh to be probed. By the first of the year even Annie started speaking hopefully about Karl's mental health, even as she herself gained strength and inner peace.

Cloris found her heart beating faster each day as she waited for Annie to come home, her fury at Clete mitigated by a scarcely acknowledged joy that he was gone from Annie's life. As the winter waned and spring approached, Annie found her laughter again. Life alone with Annie was everything Cloris had ever wanted. Feeling her curled next to her in the small bed as Annie slept gave her a solace her agitated soul had never before known.

(August 1946)

Cloris scanned Opal's letter, tossed it on the kitchen table, and poured herself some tea from the large jar where it had been brewing since morning. She took a sip, then added a partial teaspoon of sugar. She shuddered and added more, feeling guilty all the while. Annie had given up sugar in her tea and coffee entirely while rationing was on, which made Cloris feel even guiltier, but did not change her behavior. Guilt was an old friend by now – as were fear and jealousy.

Since Clete had married Oleta six years before, Cloris had fluctuated between the fierce joy of having Annie to herself and a relentless fear that Annie would leave her. The swish of Annie's skirt as she walked past still nearly made her swoon and her heart would race at the sound of Annie's gentle voice when she entered the apartment at the end of the day. When a man would ask Annie out, as they frequently did, Cloris always held her breath, fearful that she would go. For the six months before he enlisted, Marshall had been a near constant suitor, but Annie had never shown any interest beyond friendship. The worst time had come during the war, in 1942, when Annie had enlisted in the Navy. She didn't tell Cloris until the day of her physical because she knew she would try to talk her out of it. Before Cloris could enlist as well, though, Annie was rejected because of a heart murmur. Since then Cloris had become ever more protective. Often she worried that Annie felt smothered by her, but could never seem to restrain herself.

Cloris walked into the back yard with her tea in one hand and a cigarette in the other. The large victory garden of the previous summer had shrunk this year, but still took up nearly half of the yard. Since Edna upstairs had been widowed, Cloris and Annie had taken over the gardening after work and on weekends, although Edna, who was nearing eighty, still did most of the canning. Their relationship had altered over the years from that of landlord and tenants to something hovering between good friends and adopted daughters. She took a last long draw on her cigarette and ground the butt into the earth before draining her glass, picking several tomatoes, and heading back inside.

Each step down into the basement lowered the temperature two or three degrees. *Stifling out there,* she thought. Glancing at the clock, she ran her hands through her short bob. Annie, who got off work an hour after Cloris, wouldn't be home for another half hour at least. Annie still walked or took the bus to work as she had during the war, even though Cloris had bought her a good used car for her twenty-sixth birthday. Tires were still in short supply and Annie insisted they save the rubber on both cars for their trips to visit Karl, who was working on a farm near Willow Creek. The equanimity of the Jordan Valley years was long gone. Once again he eschewed the company of anyone other than Clete or Annie.

Annie worried about him constantly.

Cloris hung over the sink, tomato in one hand and salt shaker in the other, and ate the tomato. She glanced out the window, lit another cigarette, and skimmed the newspaper with restless eyes. Each minute dragged out longer than the one before. At last she heard Annie's footsteps and held open the door.

Small beads of perspiration lined Annie's flushed face, which was framed by damp, limp curls.

Cloris brushed the hair away from Annie's cheek. "You need to put your hair up on a day like today. Sit down and I'll pour you some cold iced tea."

Annie collapsed into the chair. "It's awful out there. It's too hot to walk home, but the smell on the bus like to have dropped me to the floor." She held the cold glass against her cheek and leaned back with her eyes closed. "Thanks, Clor."

Cloris rested her cigarette temporarily in the ashtray and went in the bedroom for a rubber band and hairbrush. Standing behind Annie she pulled her hair up away from her neck and face into a ponytail and secured it with the band. Her eyes still closed, Annie reached up and took Cloris's hand and squeezed it. "You are too good to me. What would I do without you?"

Sitting back down, Cloris knocked the ashes from her cigarette and resumed smoking.

"How can you smoke that thing when it is so blistering hot outside?"

Cloris slowly exhaled, her chin lifted skyward. "I will give it up when I find anything, I mean *anything,* that gives me this much pleasure."

Annie laughed and went into the bedroom to change out of her office clothes. "Who's the letter from?"

Cloris picked up the letter between her thumb and forefinger and dangled it like a dead mouse. "Opal."

"Anything new?" Annie walked back out buttoning a pale

blue gingham house dress.

"Yeah. She wants us to drive out next Saturday – for the twins' third birthday. At Clete and Oleta's, no less. Karl's invited too. Good old Opal. She doesn't miss a beat." Cloris set the letter down. "I'll tell her we're busy."

Annie leaned on the doorjamb and waited until Cloris met her eyes. "It's all right, Cloris. I got over him a long time ago. It's been six years, for Pete's sake. Tell her we'll go."

Cloris snuffed the butt in the ashtray and shook another cigarette out of the pack. She cleared her throat. "A manager's position opened up at the main office in Portland."

Annie's face clouded. "I won't leave Karl. You know that."

Cloris darted a glance at the screen door and lowered her voice. "I just thought it'd be nice to be together without living in a goddamned basement. In a big city . . ."

In the shapeless cotton dress, her hair pulled up, her face forlorn, Annie looked more like a lost child than a grown woman. "In a big city I would die." Annie picked Cloris's discarded dress off the bed and hung it in the closet. "The only thing keeping me in this city is you, Clor. Don't you know that? But I don't want to hold you back. If it's really a great promotion maybe you should take it."

Cloris' stomach lurched and panic shoved against her chest. She fought to keep her voice even. "There will be other promotions. Too damned many trees there anyway. I'll go pick us some corn for supper."

Chapter 14
Cloris and Annie:
Forms of Grief

(August, 1971)

Cloris stared off into space for several minutes before resuming her story. "We went to the birthday party and I wish to God we hadn't. I've gone over it so many times. Without us there maybe the boys would've been watched closer and maybe they'd be grown men now. Or, if Karl hadn't been there, maybe he wouldn't have gone round the bend and Annie would've stayed here. If Annie had stayed here, maybe she'd still be alive. So many 'if only's.'

"But we were there and it did happen. I hope I never have to live through anything like that again – and I barely knew my nephews. I don't know how Clete and Oleta survived it. Annie and I went back to Boise, but we were both real worried about Clete and Oleta. Of course, we didn't really know Oleta, still don't for that matter, but nevertheless we hurt for her, for both of them.

"All our lives were upended that day by the river. After the boys died Annie and I needed to do something to help, so we came up with this plan to drive to Vale every other weekend so I could take Clete out fishing or hiking, or into town for a bit, anything to take his mind off his loss for a few hours. Our plan was for Annie to do some cooking and baking the day before to send with me so she would feel like she was contributing, and she would spend her time with Karl. What we didn't count on when we made all these plans was the change in Karl."

*****

(September 1946- February 1947)

Shortly after the junction with Highway 20 the familiar outline of Malheur Butte loomed behind the stooped bodies of pickers harvesting onions in the mid-morning heat. The pungent onion-scented air stirred by a warm September wind forced them to quickly roll up the windows until they'd passed the onion fields. They sweated in silence until they could open the windows again. The grave stillness in the car was in marked contrast to the playfulness of the same trip a few weeks before.

As they rounded the last curve, the hot springs swimming pool appeared on the left, backed against the brown hillside. Annie glanced at Cloris as they crossed the Malheur River and entered the town.

"Even the town looks sad, don't you think?" Annie asked.

Cloris scanned the dusty old buildings, noted the peeling paint, the faded signs. "It's always looked like hell, Annie." She breathed in the oppressive air. "But, yeah, it seems worse now."

The road to Willow Creek, where Karl was working on a large farm, took them past the barren cemetery clinging to the side of a hill. They continued without speaking the last five miles to the farm. Karl was staying in a decaying bunkhouse behind the main farmhouse. Cloris dropped Annie at the road and made a U-turn, heading back through Vale and out to Clete and Oleta's farm.

The day felt endless. Clete puttered in the barn cleaning equipment that didn't look all that much in need of cleaning. Oleta worked in the garden with Clark, tending plants that didn't really need to be tended. It took all of Cloris's powers to cajole Clete into going into town for a drink and a game of pool. He had not even finished his whiskey by the time the second person came up to him to offer condolences. He insisted on leaving before they even picked up their cues. Back at the farm, Clark was playing quietly in the front yard trying to make trucks out of hollyhock wheels. Oleta was lying down. Cloris helped Clark with his makeshift trucks, engaged in monosyllabic conversations with Clete, and stroked the cats sprawled on the front steps. The minutes inched by.

When it became apparent that Oleta was going to do nothing about dinner, even though it was after 1:00, Cloris put Annie's casserole in the oven and shelled some peas and sliced some tomatoes to go with it. Dinner was a mostly silent affair, other than the conversation she carried on with Clark. Oleta had drifted outside with Clark, Bob trailing behind them, when Annie appeared at the screen door.

Cloris took in Annie's stricken face, her dusty wrinkled dress and filthy shoes. "What happened? Why aren't you with Karl?"

Annie's eyes filled. "He's gone, Cloris. Mrs. Maugham said he hasn't been around for over two weeks. She said he didn't say a word, didn't collect his wages, just disappeared. Clete, do you know where he is?"

Clete hunched in his chair, his hands clasped between his legs, head down. "I haven't seen him since . . ."

Cloris helped Annie into a chair at the cramped little table in the corner of the kitchen. "We'll find him, Annie. Let me get you some coffee first and then we'll talk it through. How on God's green earth did you get here?"

"I walked most of the way into town, then hitched a ride out to the turnoff with a trucker headed to Burns." She looked at Cloris out of tormented eyes. "I should never have left him here alone. I should have been here to help him."

Clete lifted his head and looked at Annie. "I walked out towards the river yesterday because. . . Hell, I don't know why, but I thought . . ." His voice broke for a moment and he hesitated before continuing on. "I thought I saw someone near that willow tree. I didn't stay long enough to know who it was, but . . ." His voice trailed off and he looked down at his hands again before pushing his chair away from the table. "I'll go and see. Maybe it's him."

Annie stood without touching her coffee. "I'm coming with you."

Cloris looked at Annie's set face and stood as well. "I'll drive." She signaled with her head toward the field outside the window. "What about Oleta?"

Clete grabbed his hat. "Hell, she don't give a damn where I am. Not now."

The car bounced along the uneven path churning up columns of dust. They left the car at the boundary to Oxman's place and walked the rest of the way to the river.

Clete stopped at the river's bank and turned to Cloris. "You should probably stay here and wait. Let me and Annie look. He might not come if he sees you."

Cloris nodded and watched until they disappeared around the bend of the river. She walked back to the car, smoking with the door open, then meandered back down to the river to cool off. Taking off her sandals she waded downstream towards a sandy bank on the opposite shore. She was nearly there when she heard a small splash coming from the far side near a cluster of Russian olive trees. As quietly as she could she waded back toward where she had left her sandals and hurried upstream to find Annie and Clete.

They were talking quietly in the shade of the two large

cottonwoods. A bedroll and knapsack were tucked into a fork in a low-lying branch of one of the trees. Annie looked worried when Cloris walked towards them.

"It's his. We're waiting for him to come back. Oh, Cloris, you need to go back to the car. You know how he is when he gets sick."

"I know, but I came to tell you I think I heard him. Downstream. Past the car."

Clete tossed the remains of his cigarette in the river and they all started back the way they had come. Cloris was prepared to drop back when they neared the car, but Karl stepped out of the willows before they had gone a hundred yards.

Annie rushed to hug him. They lingered there on the bank of the river, her arms wrapped around his emaciated frame. In one hand he clutched a fishing pole and tackle box and in the other hand he held a line from which a pair of rainbow trout dangled.

Cloris's initial reaction was to scurry away so he wouldn't be spooked, but since he showed no sign of alarm, she stayed.

"Nice fish." Clete spoke softly and calmly. "We saw your bedroll." He reached over and took Karl's fishing gear.

Karl began walking upstream towards the clearing by the cottonwoods.

They walked in silence, Annie clinging to Karl's free hand with both of hers. When they reached the clearing Karl pulled a knife from his knapsack and, squatting at the edge of the river, began gutting the fish. The other three looked at one another, but no one spoke.

Finally, Annie knelt down by Karl and laid a hand on his arm. "Karl, Mrs. Maugham said you haven't been back to your place for a while."

Karl continued working on the fish without looking up. "Can't go back. Have to stay here. Keep watch."

"Keep watch for what, Karl?"

Karl rinsed the fish and laid them on the log, then began

gathering up dried brush and piling it up. Annie looked help-lessly at Cloris and Clete. Cloris had never felt more useless.

Clete silently helped Karl with his fire, taking the knife and cutting a sturdy willow branch to hold the two fish. Karl rigged up a support to hold the fish-laden branch over the fire and lit the brush.

Clete cleared his throat. "You don't have to watch any-more, Karl." His voice caught. "They're safe now." Karl turned the fish over the fire then jumped up and paced ner-vously down to the water, back to the fire, back to the water. "Need to watch," he said, and headed off downstream.

Clete kneaded his hat with his hands, then his shoulders began to heave. Before Cloris could move Annie put her arms around him and he grabbed her like a life raft. He buried his head in her chest and sobbed. Cloris stood behind him patting him awkwardly before taking over the cooking of the fish, which had begun to burn.

Once Clete regained his composure he rummaged in Karl's bag and found a tin plate, mug, and fork. They laid the fish on the plate and waited more than an hour until Karl returned, mumbling to himself.

Annie got him to sit down on the log and eat the cold fish, but she could not get him to leave with them. As the afternoon dragged into evening Annie became increasingly agitated and all of them were sweaty, tired, and miserable. Karl kept glanc-ing anxiously downriver.

"I've got to get back to milk the cows." Clete stood and touched Karl on the shoulder. "I'll come back later."

Karl stood abruptly and headed downstream again.

Annie looked ready to collapse. Cloris took her arm and guided her towards the car. Clete stopped at the bend of the river. "I'm heading back across the fields. I need to do some thinking."

Annie cast him a desperate look. "We can't just leave him here! We can't!"

Clete stared down at his shoes. "I'll take care of him. I've got an old tent and some camping stuff. I'll bring them over tonight with some things to eat. He's been bad before. This'll pass." He put his hat on and walked off across the dry fields.

Annie did not want to drive back to Boise, but they were not prepared to camp, nor did they want to stay with Opal lest she ferret out the reason. Annie was adamant that no one know about Karl. She wanted to at least buy him some supplies, but the stores were already closed and the next day was Sunday so nothing would be open. At last she gave up and agreed to drive back to Boise as long as they returned early the next Saturday morning.

The following Saturday they left at dawn, arriving at the river early in the morning. The trunk was filled with supplies for Karl – a kerosene lamp, camp stove, bucket, tarp, towels, matches, books and magazines, and bags of food. Annie dropped Cloris at the Algood farm and talked with Clete. Karl was no better, although he was using the tent Clete had delivered. Clete checked on him daily and took him fresh vegetables from the garden.

When Annie picked up Cloris later in the day she was subdued but not distraught like the week before. They camped out that night, returning to the Malheur the next morning. Cloris stayed at the river's bend soaking her feet and reading a book until Annie returned. Annie said little on the drive home, just stared out the window in silence. As soon as they arrived home she went inside and curled up on the bed.

The temperature dropped that night and the next day was one of those dead perfect autumn days. Cloris had been home for half an hour and was waiting in the front yard under the big walnut tree for Annie to get off work. They had not discussed much the night before, but Cloris assumed they would fall into a routine of spending weekends in Vale until Karl improved enough to go back to ranch work. Karl's mental health had always been precarious, so she figured this was but another episode to be weathered.

When Annie came down the street from the bus stop, she walked with a spring in her step, as though some of the baggage that had weighed her down for the past week had been lifted. She set her purse on the top step and sat down in the lawn chair next to Cloris.

"You look perkier," Cloris said.

"I am. I made a decision today and it lifted a huge weight off my shoulders. I gave my boss two-weeks' notice today."

"What do you mean you gave notice? What are you talking about?"

"I gave my two weeks' notice. I'm going to Vale to take care of Karl."

Cloris reeled. "You're going to take care of Karl," she repeated acidly. "And how in the hell are you going to do that?"

"Cloris, don't get angry. It's only for a little while. Until he gets better."

"Are you out of your goddamned mind? You're going to stay out there on the river with him?"

"No, of course not. I'll get a place in town and find a job. But I'll be there to help him when he needs it." She glanced at the front window where Edna was peering out. "I think we'd better go inside," she whispered.

They entered the cool basement and Cloris closed the two open windows before wheeling around and facing Annie, who had taken a seat at the kitchen table. "Tell me, when you were concocting this grand scheme, did you ever, once, think about me? Or just your goddamned crazy-as-a-loon brother?"

"Please, Cloris," Annie looked up with beseeching eyes. "Anyway, it's only temporary, just until he gets back on his feet. And we can still see each other when you come to see Clete." The end of the last sentence was accompanied by a cheerful smile.

Cloris felt as though she had been kicked in the stomach. "Eight years, Annie. We've been living together for eight years. And it didn't occur to you that maybe this was a decision we should make together?"

Annie's equanimity never faltered. She looked at Cloris's pained face and held both her hands in hers. "I knew if I brought it up that you would try to talk me out of it. But it's something I have to do. I have no choice."

Cloris pulled her hands free. "Oh, you sure as hell had a choice. And you made it." She grabbed her hat off the table and opened the door. "Don't wait up."

She stayed out until the bars closed. When she stumbled into the house she was so drunk she could barely stand and so sick the next morning that she stayed home from work. Annie was unfailingly sweet and sympathetic, which only added to her misery. She wanted some sense from Annie that the decision had been an agonizing one, that leaving Cloris, even for a while, was devastating to her. Instead, Annie exuded a peaceful tranquility. Nagging away at her was the fear that Annie would never come back, in fact did not want to come back.

The next Friday Annie left for Vale for the weekend immediately after work, carrying with her camping equipment for the weekend, another casserole for the Algoods, and more food and a warm quilt for Karl. Cloris refused to go with her. Instead she left on a solitary two-day fishing trip in the Sawtooth Mountains, chain-smoking her way through two cold, miserable, alcohol-fueled days with only two small trout to show for it. She returned Sunday afternoon to an empty house.

When she saw that Annie had not yet returned, the fear she had been suppressing for a week clawed its way to the surface. She unpacked her gear, put two potatoes in to bake, and prepared the fish for frying. When the potatoes came out of the oven, she began to pace. It was long after dark before Cloris heard the crunch of tires on the gravel.

Annie opened the door with a tired smile and wrapped her arms around Cloris's waist. "How was the fishing?"

Cloris twisted away from Annie's embrace. "How was the fishing?" Cloris fought her fury. "How was the fishing? Like you give a rat's ass how the fishing was – or how I am, for that matter."

"Cloris, don't be like that." She looked around at the two place settings at the table and the cold potatoes. "Oh. You made supper. I'm so sorry. Time got away from me. I didn't mean to be so long, really."

Cloris sat at the table smoking.

"I found a place to live."

Cloris choked back her anger. "Oh. Where?"

"Remember that old bunkhouse that Virgie Condon turned into an apartment for her daughter June and her baby when Ben was off fighting in the war? Well, it's been sitting empty for a couple of years, so she's going to let me stay there for as long as I need to and she won't even let me pay rent. Three bookcases, full of books. Can you believe it? And she told me that Mr. Dentinger is looking for someone to do bookkeeping work for him part-time at Dentinger's Feed & Seed. I'm going to write to him tomorrow and ask about it. With no rent to pay and the money I've saved up, I know I can support me and Karl."

"And how is Karl?" Cloris asked with exaggerated politeness.

Annie shot her a look. "Don't, Cloris. Don't make this harder."

"Harder, Annie? Harder is not possible." She sighed. "Let me fry up this fish for us. The potatoes are gone, but we can have it with tomatoes and squash."

The rest of the week passed in a haze. On Saturday morning she watched as Annie drove off with all of her worldly goods stowed in the trunk and a promise from Cloris to visit the next weekend.

Autumn froze into winter and still Karl refused to leave the river. Shortly before Thanksgiving Annie bought a truckload of lumber and she and Clete helped Karl build a rustic one-room cabin and an outhouse in the clearing. Cloris found a used pot-bellied stove in Boise and Clete made several trips up into the mountains for wood so Karl would not freeze when the deep cold set in.

Cloris came each weekend, without fail. She vowed to herself that she would stay away, see if Annie missed her, but the ache of Annie's absence was too great and she always gave in. She would spend Saturdays with Clete, Saturday night and Sunday with Annie. Every week she left feeling more bereft than she had when she arrived. Annie always acted glad to see her, but never truly hungry for her. With each week that passed, Cloris felt the distance between them grow and swell. Annie's absence took on a form more real than the sterile days that encompassed her life.

Sometime after the holidays, even that changed. Annie's demeanor changed. She found excuses why Cloris shouldn't come. One week it would be a head cold; another she would be working all weekend. When Cloris did visit, Annie was quiet and remote. In all the years they had known one another they had never had trouble talking. Now one awkward silence followed another. When the letter came in late February asking her not to visit her again, Cloris read the words, recognizing them as ones she had read before in Annie's face.

******

(August 1971)

"Well, I did what she asked and tried to stay away. Annie had been the center of my life since I was a little girl; I didn't know how to go through the motions without her. I started going over to see Clete every other weekend, partly because things were so bad with Oleta and him, but more so I could be near Annie, maybe run into her accidentally or hear about her every now and then. It was doubly hard because I couldn't talk to anybody about it, couldn't pour my heart out into anyone's ear. I had woven my life around Annie. Who would I have talked to? I wrote to her, letter after letter, but she never answered. Not even once. Clete and I had been going fishing most Sundays since the season opened up in the spring and he had told me about how bad it was with Oleta, that he thought she was as crazy as Karl. He even talked about getting a divorce or maybe having to commit her if she kept getting worse. It was rough. We were closer than we had been for years and I thought, maybe, since he'd confided in me, maybe he might understand what I was going through.

"What an ass I was. You'd think I would have been smarter than that. We were out fishing the Owyhee when I brought it up. I don't even remember what I said, something about loving Annie and being in pain, and he stopped me cold and asked me if I was a God-cursed sodomite. Jesus. Can you imagine? I tried to explain how I felt, but he just looked at me like I was an insect. He cut me off mid-sentence and said, 'Let's get the hell out of here.'"

Cloris was interrupted by the ringing of the phone. Cass got up to answer it. Mae took the pitcher of iced tea out of the fridge and set it on the table. "Tea, Cloris?"

"Yeah, sure."

Mae grabbed four glasses from the drain board on the counter, filled them with ice, and brought them over. Cass walked back into the room.

"That was Clark. Your Mom wants you home. He sounded done in."

Mae and Jean looked at one another before Jean answered. "We'll leave after we finish our iced tea. What happened then, Cloris?"

Cloris set down her half-empty glass of tea. "He didn't say a word all the way home. When we pulled into their farm, he jumped out of the car before it came to a full stop, slammed the door, and headed into the house without looking back." Cloris took off her glasses and rubbed her eyes. "I'm shot and I've said more than I should have already. You girls need to head on home and I need to go lie down."

"Wait, Cloris." Mae put out a hand to stop her from rising. "You can't stop there. "

Cloris climbed two steps and leaned over the banister, looking at Mae and Jean. "There's not much more I can tell you. I know how the story ends, but I can't tell you a damned thing about the middle. I shouldn't have told you this much. Jesus Christ! What was I thinking? Damned wine."

Mae persisted. "But who could we talk to? Surely someone knows what happened."

Cloris sighed. "I'm not sure how much she knows, but a visit to Virgie Condon might be a good place to start."

Chapter 15
Jean and Mae

The last glimmer of daylight backlit the hills to the west as Mae backed out of Cass's driveway. The deserted town was as still as an empty movie set.

Jean stretched her arm out the window to catch the breeze as they drove through town. "I love this time of day in the high desert. Warm, but not too warm. Still a little light and the hills stand out against the sky. Pretty soon we'll hear the coyotes and later the Milky Way will come out and light up the sky."

"Stars and coyotes are fine, but I had enough of this place growing up. Give me fir trees and blackberry bushes." Mae rested her arm on the window. "I was planning to leave Tuesday, but I think I'm going to let my boss know I need another week or two. I'm not leaving here before we talk to Virgie and whoever else we need to talk to and get a few answers."

"Mae, are you all right?"

"Yeah. A little in shock. You know, I actually used to daydream about finding out that I was adopted? Of course, in my daydreams my real mother was usually an American nurse who fell in love with a British RAF officer who died tragically. That was the basic story, but the rest of it changed from day to day. I guess I got the unwed mother part right. You know what's weird? I feel more connected to Mom than I ever have and less to Dad. You'd think it would be the opposite – after all, he's part of my blood and she isn't."

"Good Lord, Mae! How can you be so calm? If he weren't already dead, I'd give the bastard a piece of my mind. How could he do something like that to Mom when she was suffering so much? Do you think it's really possible that she doesn't know? What did he do, walk up to the door holding you and say, 'Hello dear, I'm home. I brought you a little something.' Holy shit."

Mae grinned. "Did my squeaky-clean little sister just let loose with a mouthful? Felt good, didn't it?"

Jean smiled ruefully. "Yeah. A little. The jackass."

"Son-of-a-bitch!" Mae shouted back.

"Goddamned hypocrite!"

"Two timing lecher!"

By this time they were both laughing uncontrollably. They had almost reached the turn-off to the farm, so Mae pulled over by the silage pit until they could get a grip.

Jean fished in her pocket for a tissue and handed one to Mae. "Man, that felt good."

"Which part, the swearing or the laughing?"

"Both." Jean daubed at her eyes. "Felt damned good. I may have to enrich my vocabulary." She looked out the window at the open silage pit lit by the full moon. "What a place to pull over. That thing stinks to high heaven. Get us out of here."

Mae started the car, then leaned over and hugged Jean. "I tell you what. I'm sure glad you're still my blood-sister. Even if you do have a foul mouth." She let up on the clutch and eased the car over the embankment and onto the narrow dirt lane leading to the house.

They heard the door slam before Mae had even turned off the car and an exceedingly drunk Oleta came stumbling out.

"Where the hell've you been? You'd think you'd wanna be

with your family steada keepin' me up waitin' on you, thinkin' you was in an accident and bleedin' in a ditch."

Mae took one side and Jean the other and together they helped her back into the house while apologizing for worrying her. Clark rose as they entered and kissed Oleta on the cheek.

"See you in the morning, Mom. I'm pooped." He leaned over and whispered in Jean's ear, "She's all yours," before heading for the cool stone room to sleep.

When Jean awoke the next day the sun was already high in the sky. The tantalizing aroma of fresh coffee permeated the house, the smell wafting into the bedroom. Muffled voices came from the kitchen. In the distance a cow was lowing, otherwise it was quiet and still, as isolated farms often are in the high desert late on an August morning. She stretched and threw on her clothes before opening the bedroom door and following the voices into the kitchen. Mae was trying unsuccessfully to get Oleta to eat.

"Mom, you can't just drink coffee all day," Mae insisted. "You have to eat something or you'll really be sick. If you don't want the ham and eggs, how about I fry up a potato for you? That always settles my stomach when I've had a little too much."

Oleta lifted her head from where it rested on her hand and smiled wanly when she spotted Jean. "Well there she is. We thought you was going to sleep all day."

Clark was sprinkling Tabasco over a mound of scrambled eggs and a large slab of ham left over from the funeral. "Morning, Jean. We've got enough leftovers here to feed a Legionnaire's convention. And I gathered up at least a dozen eggs this morning, so there's plenty if you want to make yourself some."

"Jean, can you get Mom to eat something? I . . ."

Jean held up her hand. "Geez. I'm still waking up. Give me a minute. "She sat down by Oleta. "How are you feeling, Mom?"

Oleta half laughed, half snorted. "Hell. I can't decide what's worse – the brass band going on in my head or the pit full of vipers writhing around in my stomach. Mae, if you get me another cup of coffee I'll try to put down some spuds."

Through the window, the roar of a tractor starting up sounded in the distance. "Is that Steve Fulmer again?" Jean asked.

Oleta looked absently out the window. "Probably. Me and Leroy had a chat yesterday. He told me Steve's willing to stay on running the place for me, at least till next spring. What he'd really like to do is to buy the place, if I decide to sell out. Leroy told me Steve thought it would be disrespectful to bring it up now, but Leroy thought it might set my mind at ease to let me know."

Jean, Mae, and Clark looked at one another. Over the past three days the future of the farm had lain heavily on all their minds.

"Do you want to sell it?" Jean asked.

Oleta rubbed her temples and looked at her daughter. "Do I want to sell it? Hells Bells! Ain't I been trapped on this goddamned farm for more than thirty years? Hell yes, I want to sell it – not that it's worth much, after what we owe the bank. If I could get off this place tomorrow, I'd do it."

Mae scraped the fried potatoes onto a plate and set it in front of her mother and began gently rubbing Oleta's back. "If you really feel that way, that's what you should do. Clark can talk to Leroy and Steve before he leaves tomorrow and get the process started, and Jean and I can help you sort through things and get you moved into town. You know Cass would love to have you stay with her until you decide what you want to do. There's no reason for you to stay out here alone."

Oleta rested her head on Mae's shoulder and quietly began to cry.

*****

The next day Clark met with Leroy and Steve and hammered out the terms of a sale. Steve and his new wife, who had been staying with Leroy and Betty, would move into the house once Oleta moved to town and take over everything, including the dog if Oleta wanted. In the end, other than the household goods, the only thing Oleta wanted was Martha, the old three-legged cat. Shep and the other cats would stay with the farm. Steve would make regular payments beginning in the fall after the harvest came in and Leroy agreed to guarantee payments. Oleta could store some things in the stone room until the next spring, or even longer if she needed. Once the agreements were in place, Oleta found staying in the house nearly intolerable. Clark left Monday morning to prepare for his high school classes that would begin the following week and Jean and Mae stayed to help Oleta sort through her things and pack.

By far the worst was retrieving the dozens of quarts and pints of home-canned tomatoes, beans, corn, pickles and jams from the root cellar. August was spider-mating season and every trip down into the cellar, even with gloves on and their heads covered with towels, was a descent into hell. They had argued with Oleta unsuccessfully to leave it all for the newlyweds, but Oleta was determined to take her hard work with her. Some of the jars were so encrusted in dirt and cobwebs that the girls were certain they had been there since the war. Even taking turns they had to gird up their loins to face it and could force themselves to make only a few trips each before calling it a day.

Wednesday was Cass's day off and she had convinced Oleta to take a break from sorting and packing to go shopping with her in Boise for some new clothes to start her life as a "city woman." Jean and Mae dropped Oleta at Cass's house on Wednesday morning. When they walked in Cloris was sitting at the dining room table, Buttons at her feet, sipping coffee and eating toast and jam with Cass.

"I thought you were going over to the Starlite Cafe with us to have biscuits and gravy," Mae said when she saw Cloris eating. Both girls leaned over and kissed Cass and smiled at Cloris.

"Hell, this isn't breakfast, it's an appetizer. I can still eat the two of you under the table. Morning, Oleta."

Mae poured herself a cup of coffee and Cass headed upstairs to get her purse. Oleta stood in the doorway in a snug print dress with a ragged white purse on her arm. The four of them made small talk until Cass came back downstairs. Cloris had spent Sunday evening with them before Clark left for home, but Oleta and Cloris were still tentative around one another. The stairs shook as Cass descended. "You ready, Oleta? I hope you've got your checkbook because you are one woman who needs some new clothes, and a new purse too, judging by the looks of that one."

Oleta patted the pocketbook dangling from her arm. "Got it right here. It's been so damned long since I had me a new dress I don't even know what's in style. Remember when I used to dress like Mae West?"

Cass looked her up and down. "Used to?"

Oleta shoved Cass lightly and Cass gave her a tight hug. Oleta's eyes filled with tears. "Hey, none of that. Let's go have some fun." Cass turned to the three sitting at the table. "I filled up Buttons' water dish out on the porch, but you make sure he gets put out when you go or he'll be leaving me a welcome home gift in the middle of the dining room rug."

After the screen door slammed behind them Mae and Cloris drank their coffee in silence.

Finally, Cloris spoke. "Cass talked to Virgie last night. She's expecting us."

After Jean put Buttons out on the porch, the three went back through the house and got into Cloris's car. Instead of heading west toward the café, they turned due south at Main Street and headed out of town towards the Condon farm.

Chapter 16
Virgie's Story

Virgie waited on the porch as they pulled into her driveway in a billow of dust, scattering a dozen hens that had been pecking along the side of the driveway. Her tidy ranch house had been spruced up with new mint green siding and the yard was a riot of color. Enormous pink dahlias drooped over petite red zinnias. Burgundy hollyhocks and lavender Rose-of-Sharon lined the fence; marigolds, petunias, and pansies jostled each other for space. A hundred yards from the house a decaying bunkhouse disappeared beneath a mound of white morning glory.

Virgie greeted them at the door, her short bulky form nearly filling the frame.

"Come on in. The bread just came out of the oven. Got to beat the heat you know. Could I get you all a warm slice with some of my good boysenberry jam?"

Virgie ushered them into the darkened living room, shades pulled to keep out the heat. Books lined every wall of the house.

"It looks just the way I would expect a librarian's house to look," Jean said.

"I've got a bookcase in every room of the house, including

the bathroom, and I still run out of room. Ed keeps telling me that we'd be wealthy people if I'd stop buying books. He probably has a point." Virgie insisted on serving everyone a hunk of warm sourdough bread with jam and hot coffee before she would sit down with them to talk. Jean doctored her coffee with three teaspoons of sugar.

Virgie watched her and laughed. "Would you like a little coffee with that sugar? Your Mom always takes it black as a witch's Sabbath."

Jean grinned sheepishly and shook her head. "So does Mae. Not me. I've got a terrible sweet tooth, I admit it."

Virgie leaned back with her cup in her hand and looked directly at Mae. "So, I guess you all want to talk about that sweet little Annie. Cass told me to tell you everything and you're grown women so I guess you've got a right to know, but don't you even think about talking to your Mom about any of this, you hear? The truth is, I don't like to think about it much myself. It still breaks my heart. I got to be so fond of that girl when she was staying here that year."

Virgie stopped to take a bite of bread. "She was so fragile, Annie was, and so gentle. Too gentle for this world, that's what I think. I've never told a soul about what happened that summer, not even my husband. I wouldn't for the world hurt your mother and what earthly good could it do for me to be spouting off? I hate to speak ill about your father, but I'll tell you, I will never forgive Clete Algood for what he did to that girl. The good Lord says we must forgive everyone and I know I'll have to account for that, but I just couldn't do it. But that's wrong and it's a sin and that's my cross to bear. If I'm going to tell you girls, and you, Cloris, about Annie, you've got to promise me not to let it turn you bitter or ruin any good memories you have of your dad."

"Good memories?" Mae said. "Those are few and far between. But I guess there were some nice moments. I'll hang on to those. Don't worry."

"The same goes for me," Jean said.

Cloris sipped her coffee and looked at Virgie. "There is nothing you could say that would make me more bitter than I already am."

Virgie looked at Cloris steadily, as if considering something. "Annie came to me in the fall of 1946. We'd fixed up the bunkhouse into a little two-room apartment for my daughter June during the war, but she'd moved out after her husband came home and they all moved to Nampa where he found a job. The bunkhouse was just sitting empty, so why not let her have it? She was such a sweet little thing and so pretty. Wavy hair the color of flax and cornflower blue eyes. And no bigger than a minute. I made three – or four—of her even then and I'm a good sight bigger now. I do love my daily bread!" Virgie patted her stomach.

"She was real worried about her brother Karl and he was the only family she had in the world. Their mother died when they were young and the father sold the farm and moved back to Minnesota after Annie graduated high school. He died two or three years later, but it didn't sound like Annie and Karl had much to do with him after he left. She and Karl had never met any of their parents' families, wherever they were. I gathered that it had always really just been Karl and Annie looking after each other, even before their father left. Mr. Mueller always kept to himself; even the neighbors hardly knew him. Something was always kind of off with him.

"Anyway, Karl had been a little strange in the head for years, maybe something ran in the family, but he went completely around the bend after the twins drowned. He was camping out there on the Malheur on the edge of your farm. She told me he was watching for the twins and wouldn't leave the river. It was real sad. Well, I thought they ought to have him committed, but she wouldn't hear of it. She said he was her brother and she would take care of him. The only time she kind of got her back up was when I suggested that, so I never mentioned it again. She wasn't really here all that much for those first six months. She went out to Karl's place nearly every day, after work if she was working, and stayed late."

Virgie turned to Cloris. "As I recall, you used to come pretty near every weekend too, for the first several months. When you stopped coming by I asked if the two of you had had some misunderstanding since you had been such close friends for so long, but Annie wouldn't talk about it. Of course, I didn't know what was going on with Clete. I didn't find that out until I forced it out of her. . . . "

*****

(May-August 1947)

Virgie had been puttering around in the flowerbeds since shortly after breakfast keeping watch out of the corner of her eye for signs of activity in the bunkhouse. She had waited until long after dark the night before with the intention of talking to Annie, but had given up before Annie came home. Now, bending over to uproot a dandelion, she thought she saw movement behind one of the curtains. She stretched her back, put the spade down, and knocked on the door. "Annie. Could I talk to you?"

"Of course, Mrs. Condon. Could you give me a minute?" On the other side of the door there were sounds of tidying up and a chair scraping over the linoleum.

"Come on in."

Annie opened the door wearing a loose apron over her dress and holding a shirt and threaded needle in front of her. "Please, come in and sit down. I'm mending one of Karl's shirts."

Virgie sat across from Annie, who seemed more pale than usual. "I stopped in at the Feed & Seed and Stan told me you weren't working there anymore and hadn't been for several weeks."

Annie reddened and looked down, stumbling through an explanation. "Well, I've got enough to last me for at least half a year and I thought maybe I could help Karl more if I wasn't tied up with work right now. Mr. Dentinger said he'd take me back whenever I was ready."

Virgie hesitated. "Like maybe after that baby's born?"

Annie turned deep scarlet and dropped the needle, averting her eyes and hugging the shirt to her.

"Annie, honey. I gave birth to seven of my own and my nineteenth grandchild is on the way. I can tell a pregnant woman when I see one. I know this isn't any of my business, but it seems to me you are in sore need of a little mothering, and that's something I'm pretty good at it."

Annie did not lift her head or look at Virgie, she just began to cry softly. Virgie knelt beside her and pulled her to her bosom.

When Annie had cried herself out, Virgie released her and struggled to rise. "I got myself down here, but I'm not sure I can get myself back up, not without a little help."

Annie helped Virgie to her feet, which gave Virgie a chance to examine her figure before she lowered herself into a chair. "I'd say you're about six months gone. Is that about right?"

"I think so."

"You're awful skinny for someone having a baby and I don't like your color. Have you been sick?"

Annie nodded. "It's been a little better the last month or so, but I can't keep much down. About the only thing I can eat is potatoes and not much of those."

"Well, the first thing that's going to happen is I'm going to bring you dinner every day. I can pick up your groceries and such for the time being too. You surely can't be going into town anymore unless you want the whole world to know. I guess you figured that out, or you wouldn't have quit work. If you're careful no one around here even needs to know. Ed hardly noticed when I was pregnant, let alone another woman."

Annie took Virgie's hands and squeezed them. "Mrs. Condon, I don't know how to thank you."

"Nonsense. I'm not doing a thing anyone else wouldn't do. You could dearly use a good friend right now. I don't pretend to know what happened between you and Cloris, but. . ."

Annie interrupted her, her face clouding. "No. Absolutely not. Cloris can't know about this. No."

"Ok. Have it your way. But there are two things we do need to talk about. The first one I think I know the answer to, but I don't like it. As I recall, you and Clete Algood were high school sweethearts. And I also recall that he and Karl were real close. I'm not good at math, but I can put two and two together. So, what I'm getting at is that I figure that Clete Algood is the one that got you in the family way. Am I right?"

Annie picked at her dress and did not look up or answer.

"I'm going to take that as a yes. I guess the main thing we need is to find you a place to go to have the baby. One of my nieces got herself in the family way in high school and my sister-in-law found a place in Portland where girls could stay until their time came. Now you might not want to go that far away, but I could do some checking and see if there's a place in Boise or . . ."

Again Annie interrupted her and stated very softly but firmly, "I'm not leaving Karl and I'm not giving the baby up. Clete will take care of us."

Virgie stared agape at Annie. "Annie, Clete is a married man. He has a family."

"He's going to get a divorce. He's never loved Oleta and he says she tricked him into marrying her anyway. When the twins died that finished off whatever they had between them. He's going to leave her as soon as Oleta starts doing better. He doesn't want to leave when she's still grieving, that's all. I know he loves me and if I'm patient, it will all work out. He promised me."

"Men promise a lot of things to get what they want. It takes a long time to get a divorce. And what if Oleta doesn't want to give him one? He was the one who broke his wedding vows. He's got no grounds for a divorce unless she agrees."

"But he does have grounds. She tricked him into marrying her and now she won't even let him touch her. That's grounds, isn't it? Anyway, I know he loves me and I love him. It will all work out. I know it will."

Virgie opened and closed her mouth, biting her tongue. "But meanwhile? You can't raise a baby alone. How would you support yourself? What would people think?"

Annie set her jaw. "People can think whatever they want. When he leaves Oleta we'll move away from here and start over where no one knows us. We'll take Karl with us and then I'll always be able to take care of him. It won't be long anyway. Maybe even before the baby is born."

Nothing Virgie could say shook Annie's faith in Clete, so she gave in and took on the role of caring for her. For a while Annie seemed to be doing better. Her color improved and she put on a pound or two with Virgie's cooking. She spent part of each day outside, when no one but Virgie was there. Working with the flowers especially delighted her and lifted her spirits. She would sit on the ground to avoid bending and weed and clip. She even planted an additional bed of dahlias in front of the bunkhouse. Shoots were just emerging when something changed.

She seemed to curl in on herself. She came home earlier from her daily trips to see Karl and only picked at the food Virgie brought. She stopped working in the flowerbeds and never stepped outside. Even though her pregnancy was progressing, she looked gaunt and worn. Finally, in late July, Virgie pulled it out of her that Clete had told her he was not leaving Oleta after all. He had told her that it had all been a mistake and she should give the baby up for adoption. He was curt and sarcastic with her and told her she should go back to

Boise, that maybe Cloris would take her in. He had stopped going by Karl's place, at least when she was there. He had abandoned her.

The next month was a nightmare for both of them. Virgie was consumed with worry for her, but Annie seemed incapable of action. Virgie found a home in Boise for unwed mothers, but Annie refused to go to Boise. The person in charge of the Boise home told her of a family in Baker that took in one girl at a time until their confinement was over and the cost was reasonable. Virgie secured the spot for her in the Baker home and offered to drive her, but Annie insisted on going alone. Twice she scheduled her departure and twice backed out on the day she was to leave. Each time Virgie got so anxious for her that she bit her nails clear down to the quick. Then, on a scorching day near the end of August, Virgie found a note that Annie had slipped under her front door, telling her she'd left for Baker that morning.

(August 1971)

"I didn't know that she never left for Baker at all until Leroy came to tell me what had happened. My guess is that when her labor started she drove on over to Karl's place. Poor thing. She was such a tiny waif and so frail. I think she didn't have much will to live at that point. I didn't find out what happened until Leroy came by two days later and told me. If it weren't for Leroy convincing me we needed to protect Oleta, I might have blabbed to the whole county. May God forgive me, but I've hated Clete Algood from that day on. We put the story out that she died of pneumonia. Karl was too far gone to come to any services, so we just had a prayer at the gravesite, me and Cloris, a few neighbors, and the priest."

Cloris had stood toward the end of Virgie's story and was staring out the big front window chewing her thumbnail. Virgie went to the kitchen for a fresh pot of coffee. When she returned Cloris sat down with her coffee and rested her chin on her crossed hands. "I was too distraught to even wonder at the time, but why did you write to tell me? If Annie had told you not to, why *did* you?"

Virgie took a sip before answering. "After Leroy left I went over to the bunkhouse to see if she had left any things. Most everything she had, what little there was of it, was still there. I didn't know what to do with the stuff, so I started in to box it up, crying my heart out all the while. Under the bed I found a box that must have had 50 letters in it, all from you.

"Something about that box full of letters struck me. For one thing, it wasn't dusty like it should have been from being under the bed. And each of those letters had that worn look, like they'd been read over and over and carefully refolded each time and put back in the envelope. A couple of them fell apart when I took them out. It reminded me of the box I have up in the attic from the boy I was in love with before Ed came along. It had that look about it. I knew I was snooping, but I did it anyway – I read some of them. I didn't quite know what to do. They were more like love letters than letters from a friend. I had read about women who loved other women that way in some of my books, but I couldn't imagine that Annie. . . Well, I brooded on it all day and did some praying and finally I decided I was imagining things that probably weren't true. And even if I wasn't imagining things, it wasn't my place to be setting myself up as a judge. I'll leave that to the good Lord to figure out. Annie deserved someone who loved her and knew the truth at that graveside. So I sent you that letter telling you she had died and asking you to come."

"But you didn't tell me the truth until I got here. Why?"

"Some things need to be told face to face. I thought you might put two and two together when you heard about Oleta's baby, and it was better it came from me."

Mae spoke for the first time since Virgie had begun her story. "Do you know how Dad did it? I have a birth certificate with Oleta's name on it. And how did he get Oleta to believe his story? None of it makes any sense."

"I can't help you there. Leroy might know, but I never heard a word about that. It's a small town and I can't believe, even all these years later, that they pulled it off without anyone knowing. Oleta loves you like her own, that's the God's truth. And I know Annie loved you too, God rest her soul."

Virgie set her cup down and turned to Cloris. "I still have her things up in the attic. Would you like to have them?"

Chapter 17
Jean and Mae:
Cleaning Up

(August, 1971)

Mae dumped the bucket of soapy brown water into the kitchen sink. "Between you and me, that bathroom is disgusting. I don't think it's been cleaned since we left home and stopped cleaning it ourselves." She wiped her hands on a dry cleaning rag and opened the fridge, standing in the door as the cool air washed over her. "Wouldn't Dad have had a fit if he could see me now, holding the refrigerator door open and wasting money." She looked at Jean, who was on her knees scouring the oven. "I don't know about you, but I need a break. Coke or iced tea?"

Jean pulled her head from inside the grease-encrusted oven. "Is there any sugar?"

"No, sorry. I packed it up with the rest of the cupboard stuff yesterday."

"Coke then, but no glass; I like it in the bottle." She stuck her head back in the oven and dislodged a stubborn charred clump. She sat back on her haunches, wiped her face with one arm, and stripped off the heavy rubber gloves.

Mae sat on the shaded front step sipping her tea and petting Shep. Loose strands of hair had escaped her braid and clung to her sweaty face. Her white t-shirt was smeared with grime and her legs and feet were bare. The near-empty tea jug that had been brewing in the sun all morning lay in the grass next to her sandals, and her opened bottle of coke sat beside her on the step. Jean kicked off her flip-flops and plopped down too. For some time the two enjoyed the cool drinks in silence. In the distance a tractor motor revved once and died. A raucous gathering of magpies chattered in the locust tree.

Oleta had left earlier with the last of her personal belongings, Martha the cat yowling at the car window. She planned to spend the rest of the day settling in at Cass's house while the girls finished cleaning the nearly empty house. Steve and his wife were planning to move in the next week and all of the larger furniture, which for the most part was old and shabby, had been left for the young couple. The stone room was half full of things she couldn't decide what to do with, but Jean and Mae considered most of it junk.

Mae sighed as she drained her glass. "*'Off of your ass, onto your feet/ Out of the shade, into the heat.'* How many times do you suppose we heard Mom say that to us when we were hoeing those damned beets?"

"Too many, that's for sure. And then she'd give us a stick of Doublemint gum. To this day I hate that gum."

"Well, time to get off our asses and back into the house or we'll never get this finished. I wish Will hadn't gone back to Boise — we could have recruited him to help us. I'll be glad to hit the road in a couple of days. I haven't worked this hard in years."

The hum of a motor caught their ears and they watched as Leroy's dented blue pickup bounced along the rutted lane bordering the drainage ditch, churning up billowing dust clouds as it approached the house. Shep flew into a barking frenzy until Leroy pulled to a stop.

"Afternoon, girls." Leroy tipped his hat to Jean and Mae and knelt down to tousle Shep's ears.

"Hello, Mr. Fulmer. You just missed Mom."

Leroy kneaded his hat in his hands. "Me and Betty passed her car on the way home from church a bit ago." He grinned shyly. "Looked like that cat was giving her a run for her money." He stared down at his boots. An awkward silence filled the empty space before he spoke again. "The thing is, I was hoping to catch you two girls alone before you left. I had me a talk with Virgie yesterday and I've been mulling it over in my head ever since. It seems to me that maybe there are some things I ought to tell you."

Mae glanced at Jean. "Come in then and let's sit down. I'm afraid the coffee pot has been packed, but there's some sun tea. Jean, will you grab that jug?" Mae nattered on. "It's a hot one, isn't it?"

Leroy nodded and sat down at the kitchen table while Jean filled a glass with ice and the last of the tea. Leroy sipped his tea, his gaze shifting from his feet to the window. Both girls waited impatiently for him to begin. He cleared his throat, but before he could speak Shep leapt off the porch in another paroxysm of barking as Cloris's old beige Volvo pulled up to the house.

All three of them stood to greet her as Mae held open the screen door.

"Well, isn't this a nice surprise. First Mr. Fulmer saves us from having to get back to work and now you come by. Can I get you a coke? We're fresh out of iced tea."

Cloris shook Leroy's hand and sat down. "I'll take anything cold. It's a son-of-a-bitch out there. I forgot how hot and muggy it gets here in August. I must have gotten soft living in Portland; I wilt like a spent flower by mid-morning. I was just out at Opal's place saying my goodbyes. I thought I'd head out tonight as soon as the sun goes down instead of waiting till tomorrow. I'm champing at the bit to get back, but it's too damn hot to drive during the day. I couldn't leave without saying goodbye anyhow."

Leroy had picked up his hat when he stood to greet Cloris and when the girls sat down he continued to stand, working the hat with his fingers. Finally, he set the hat on the stove, the only free surface other than the table, and looked directly at Cloris.

"I come on out to talk to Jean and Mae, but I reckon you've got a right to hear what I'm going to tell them, if you've got the time."

Cloris frowned and shifted in her chair. "I've got as long as I want to have. Sit down, Leroy. Tell us what's on your mind."

Chapter 18
Leroy's Piece of the Story

(August 23, 1947)

A moist trickle of sweat ran down Leroy's face and his soggy shirt clung to his back as he stepped out of his dusty truck. That morning he had dropped Betty and the boys off at her mother's place to spend the last few weeks of her pregnancy and had decided to check on Clete and Oleta for the first time in over a month. Since the pastor's sermon the week previous, his neglect of his neighbors had weighed on him. Even though it was barely mid-morning the air was sultry and oppressive, hinting of storm. Leroy pulled open the creaky gate and looked over the front yard with a pang of guilt. Since he had last come by in mid-July the unwatered flowers in the front yard had withered and died and the lawn had become a brown stubble field.

Leroy heard Clark's voice coming from the back yard and walked around the corner of the house. Clark was sitting at the edge of the vegetable garden with a mason jar of water carefully forming mud pies. Already he had five lined up in a neat row next to the pole beans.

Leroy squatted next to Clark. "Looks like you've got dinner about ready."

Clark looked up solemnly. "This isn't dinner. This is just pretend pies. Mama makes dinner."

Leroy chuckled. "You got me there. Where is your mama, anyway?"

"She's lying down. She has a headache, so I have to play real quiet so I don't hurt her head."

"What about your daddy? Does he have a headache too?"

"Only Mommies get headaches." Clark continued shaping the mud pie, stray bits of mud plopping on his bare legs.

"Is Bob with your daddy?"

Clark looked around for a minute before refocusing on the mud, setting the pie down next to the others and smearing the clumps on his leg. "Bob helps Daddy to herd the cows."

Leroy stood and looked off into the distance. "Well, you tell your mama I stopped by. Can you do that for me?

"Ok."

Leroy climbed up the embankment above the drainage ditch, to where he could see most of Clete's fields, and called Clete's name. There was no sign of either Clete or Bob, so Leroy figured he must be over at the river visiting Karl. For the past year Karl had done occasional work for Leroy, the few times he was stable enough, and Leroy had pitched in to help set him up in the small shack once it became clear that Karl would not leave. It nagged at him that he hadn't told Betty about Karl. It was the only real secret he had kept from her in their married lives, but he knew she would push to have Karl committed to the state hospital, or worse yet rally the women to help. Leroy couldn't stand the thought of that timid soul being hounded by a clutch of well-meaning women.

Mostly, though, he had been troubled by Annie's continued presence. Something about the way she and Clete acted around each other set off alarm bells. He hated to even think such a thing about a friend and neighbor, but he knew in his soul that the infrequency of his visits since spring were more a result of fear over what he might learn about Clete than the pressing chores on his own land. Leroy took off his hat and patted his face with his handkerchief. His initial thought had been to walk across the fields, but the punishing heat caused him to drive via the rutted dirt track adjacent to Oxman's spread.

The Malheur ran wide and shallow where he parked in the partial shade of a copse of willows. He splashed his face and neck with the cool water and lapped up a handful before following the well-worn path north to Karl's shack. Three vultures circumscribed ever-widening arcs in the cloudless expanse overhead. The stench of a rotting animal carcass nearby mingled jarringly with the pleasant tang of sage. As he neared the shack he was brought up short by a piercing animal wail. He stopped and listened. The sound ceased, then began again, rising to a higher pitch. Horrified, Leroy realized that it was not an animal cry that he heard, but a human one.

Running now, he rounded the bend in the river and found Clete sitting on the log outside Karl's shack, rocking back and forth and keening. Bob paced around him whining frantically. Leroy put his hands on Clete's shoulders. "Is it Karl? Clete, answer me." Clete did not look up, just doubled up with his arms folded across his chest, rocking. Leroy rested a trembling hand on Clete's back for a moment and bent down to calm Bob. His first thought was that Karl had laid hands on himself. The menacing shack loomed over them. Leroy braced himself, took a deep breath, and pushed open the door.

A fetid odor permeated the airless room. Karl sat motionless on a wooden chair next to a bed on which Annie lay, drained of all color. Karl held her tiny hand in both of his, a distant look in his eyes. A pool of blood had spread from the bed to the wall and a bloody blanket lay crumpled on the floor. Next to the bed a suitcase lay open, its contents, mostly diapers and baby clothes, spilling out onto the floor. Some of the clothes had soaked up the leading edge of blood like a sponge.

Leroy's heart pounded and he fought the gorge rising in his throat. He focused on the locket around her neck as he felt for a pulse. Finding none, he put a quivering hand on Karl's shoulder. "Karl, what happened here?"

Karl did not respond. Leroy squatted down and shook him gently by the shoulders, calling his name until Karl looked at him.

"Annie's looking for Joey and Jimmy. We've got to find them." His eyes drifted away as he stroked Annie's hair.

Leroy backed up, stumbling over a bloody towel. Another wave of nausea washed over him and he struggled against the overwhelming urge to flee. The pounding of his own heart deafened him. Reeling, he backed against a wall, closing his eyes to regain his composure and make sense of what he was seeing. As he stood there fighting for breath he heard a faint mewling sound, such as a small kitten might make. He scanned the room, following the sound to the other side of the bed. Facing down the rising panic, he stepped carefully around the opened suitcase and the blood-soaked clothes and found a tiny baby not more than a few hours old. It was wrapped in a cotton blanket and lay in a chipped porcelain washbasin atop a ragged towel.

The sight of the baby, which had been carefully wrapped in the blanket, swept away Leroy's panic. He bent down and unwrapped the baby, setting off a healthy wail. She was dressed in a simple cotton gown and a diaper. Leroy lifted the gown and saw that someone had tied and cut the cord. Both the diaper and the towel beneath were soaked through with urine, so Leroy made a bed of the clothes that had not been fouled with blood on which to lay the baby. After changing and rewrapping the infant, he nestled her against his shoulder, as he had his own children, cooing to her and swaying. She settled immediately.

He felt as though he had opened a door and walked into a nightmare. Again he fought the impulse to flee. Clete's wailing had stopped, but Leroy found no solace in the silence. Karl continued to sit silently stroking Annie's hands and hair.

Leroy returned the sleeping baby to the porcelain tub and wiped his dripping brow. He looked at Karl, considered briefly, then picked up the tub and took it with him, setting it down gently in the shade beside the log. Bob sniffed the baby and lay down beside her, resting his head lightly on the edge of the tub. Clete did not lift his head.

Leroy tried to still the pounding in his head and chest. "What happened here, Clete?"

Clete's shoulders shook, but no sound escaped him. At last he choked out, "I killed her, Leroy. I killed her." Clete broke down in spasmodic weeping.

Leroy tore at the skin next to his thumbnail. He weighed Clete's words before clearing his throat to speak. "I'm no doctor, but it looks to me like that girl died in childbirth, Clete. It happens sometimes."

Clete looked around wildly, choking and spitting out his words. "No, Leroy, no, goddammit! Don't try to ease it for me. This was my fault. All of it." He put his head between his legs and continued to speak even as he fought back sobs. "I loved her all my life, but I was so goddamned cocky! I didn't know what I had. So I took up with Oleta, and that was wrong, but I should have done right by both of them. I shouldn't have taken up with Annie again. I should have left her alone. But I was lonely and hurting and feeling sorry for myself. I never really thought about her. I didn't let myself think about it, any of it. Hell, I don't know what I thought – that I could have them both, even with a baby coming? Jesus Christ! And then when I found out about her and . . . ." He stopped for a few minutes to regain composure. "Maybe she didn't even . . . . . But I thought. . . ."

Another sob escaped him. "Hell, I didn't think at all. I turned on her, Leroy. I turned on her! I thought she'd go back to Boise and Cloris could deal with it, clean up my mess." He paused. "No, that's not what I thought. It's what I hoped. But she didn't go back; she just gave up – and I should have known she would." He sat with his head in his hands. "And now she's dead and it ain't nobody's fault but my own." His voice quavered. "My boys are dead and that's a good part my fault too. And Oleta's back at the house broken and that's laying at my door." He began to rock and moan again. "Oh, God, O God!"

Leroy waited until Clete was quiet again. The river bubbled next to them. Far in the distance a dog barked. Bob lifted his head for a minute before laying it back down again next to the baby. "Clete, I need you to tell me what happened here, before I come out."

Clete pinched his eyes with his fingers. His hand shook. "I was cleaning out the barn this morning after the milking and Karl come in, looking wild-eyed and frantic. He was scared, but there wasn't nothing crazy about him. He said for me to come, that Annie was at his place and that she had had a baby and she was real sick. I dropped the shovel and ran straight over here with him." Clete broke down again before regaining his composure. "She was already dead when I got here." Clete glanced up at the sun. "That must have been a couple of hours ago. And Karl. . . " Clete began rocking again, holding his arms to his sides.

"Clete, who cleaned up that little girl? Was that you?"

Clete looked around blankly. "Girl? It was a girl?"

"Yes, a girl. She's sleeping right here."

Clete's face drained of any remaining color and he looked around, his eyes finally resting on the washbasin under the tree. "Sleeping? It's alive?"

Leroy sat down beside him on the log. "Not 'it', Clete. Her. Somebody cleaned her up and dressed her and wrapped her in a blanket. Annie must have done it before she sent Karl to get you." He paused to compose his thoughts again.

"Clete, you've got to get a grip on yourself. You can't bring Annie back. Some things you can't ever undo. Those things are between you and God. "Leroy jumped up and paced. "But maybe there's a way you can fix what you done to Oleta. As I understand it, Annie and Karl don't have no other family living. Is that right?" Clete nodded his assent. "Well, this here's your little girl and she needs a mama and over yonder at your house is a woman grieving her dead babies. Seems to me . . . ."

Clete lifted his head and stared at Leroy. "I tell Oleta about that baby it'd kill her."

Leroy pivoted and exploded. "That little girl isn't just some baby. It's your daughter, goddammit!" Leroy struggled for composure. "What if you didn't tell her?" He turned around and faced Clete. "Don't tell her anything she don't need to know, especially not if it'd hurt her worse. Make up something. Say it's your cousin's baby. Say Doc Nelson had a teenage mother got herself in a fix and thought of Oleta. Hell, tell her anything. Clete, the state she's in, she won't care where this baby come from."

Clete looked at the baby sleeping in the basin and broke down in another silent bout of weeping. After a few minutes he wiped his eyes with his sleeve. "Doc Nelson ain't going to lie about this. He hates my guts and he makes that real clear. And that smug little shit that he's got taking over for him sure as hell won't. This'll be all over Vale tomorrow. Jesus."

"It don't have to be. Clete, Oleta's had enough pain to last a lifetime. Now you and Doc Nelson might not have any love lost between you, but he delivered every one of your boys and maybe even you and Oleta too. He loves Oleta and he's not one to abide by the rules if it means someone he cares about gets hurt. I'll talk to Doc Nelson."

In the washtub the baby began to stir and Bob whined and

looked at Clete anxiously. Clete stared at the baby for a brief moment then lifted her out of the tub, cradling her against his chest and stifling a sob. "Tell me what to do, Leroy. I'll do it."

Dust billowed behind him as Leroy bounced down the dirt road. The small baby, red from crying and once again swaddled tightly, lay in a tool bag on the passenger seat. Leroy had dumped the tools into the truck bed and lined the bag with the extra diapers he'd found in the suitcase. After a brief stop at his house to get baby bottles, clothes, and blankets from the room Betty had prepared for her baby, he had sped toward town, windows down to move the air. In the distance he heard the first peal of thunder. As he drove he tried to think. He needed help and he couldn't ask Betty. He loved his wife, but he didn't trust her to keep something like this from slipping out. She loved gossip too much. He could think of only one person who loved Oleta enough to do what needed to be done, and that was Cass.

He walked up to Cass's house carrying the tool bag tucked firmly under his arm. Two little girls were playing in the front yard next door. He uttered a silent prayer that the sleeping baby, who had cried most of the way to town, would not waken again until he was inside. He opened the screen door, called out Cass's name, and stepped inside.

Cass peeked her head around the doorframe from the kitchen. "Leroy? Come in and sit down. This is a surprise." She came out, wiping her hands on a dishtowel, and perused Leroy's pale face in alarm. "What's wrong? Did something happen to Oleta?"

Leroy looked hard at the young widow as though sizing her up. They were acquainted, as was nearly everyone in town, but he only knew her through Oleta. Leroy set the bag down, and carefully lifted out the baby. "Cass, I need your help."

* * * * *

Doctor Nelson was seventy-eight years old and had been

the town's only physician for longer than most people could re-member. After the war ended a young doctor who had served with Doctor Nelson's grandson had taken over his practice, and Doctor Nelson, or Doc as his patients and friends called him, only saw the occasional patient who refused to see the new doctor. Cass called him at home and woke him from a nap, telling him she had dislocated her shoulder and needed his help. As they waited in the stuffy parlor, shades drawn and windows closed, for him to walk the half block to Cass's home, she and Leroy rehashed the plan they had worked out. Cass struggled to get the baby to take the bottle.

"Are you sure about Opal?" Leroy chewed off a piece of thumbnail and spit it out the corner of his mouth.

"I know a few things about Opal. She's smart, and even though she doesn't look it, she's tougher than any cowboy I ever met. And most important, she loves her brother. Annie grew up in this town and people will want to know what hap-pened to her. Whatever story gets put out, Opal would put two and two together anyway. On top of which, one of us needs to stay here out of sight and take care of this little girl until this gets resolved one way or the other, and someone else is going to have to go help with Karl and, well, the mess. I can't be in two places, Leroy. But if we can't talk Doc Nelson into going along with this, which is a long shot, there won't be much to talk to her about anyway."

"Here he is now." Leroy picked up his hat reflexively and stepped out on the porch to greet the doctor.

"Howdy, Doc."

Doctor Nelson gave Leroy a puzzled look. "Leroy. I didn't expect to find you here."

Leroy held open the door for the doctor and followed him in. Doc Nelson raised his eyebrows as Cass greeted him, the baby in her arms. "That dislocated shoulder seems to have put itself right while I was walking over." He looked from Leroy to Cass to the baby and back at Leroy.

Cass swayed to soothe the baby, who was again starting to fuss. "I'm sorry about lying to you, Doc. I was afraid to tell you anything over the phone. You know how Lillian is always listening in on the line. Sit down and I'll get you some coffee and we'll explain everything."

* * * * *

Doc Nelson swaddled the squalling baby and handed her back to Cass. "She's small, but she looks healthy enough. Sponge her off later with some warm water, no soap. You got any cans of evaporated milk?" He wiped his sweaty neck with his handkerchief.

"Yeah, I think so," Cass replied.

"Give it to her. You want a colicky baby, keep doing what you're doing. Put a drop of honey on that nipple and she'll take it. You think you can handle her till tomorrow when we straighten this all out?"

Cass started to speak, but Doc interrupted her, turning to Leroy.

"Leroy, I'll follow you out in my station wagon. We can bring Annie back in that."

Leroy stood and looked down at his feet for a moment. "So you'll do it?"

"Leroy, what you're asking me to do is against the law. Do you know that? You could get all of us thrown in jail."

"Yes, sir. I guess I do." He looked the doctor directly in the eye. "But there's man's law and there's a higher law. Cass and me, well, we think maybe this is one of those times to listen to that higher law."

"Goddamm it, Leroy. Spare me the moralizing. I'm not promising a damned thing. Jesus Christ, what a mess! I'm too old for this shit." Doc picked up his hat and put it on.

"Sorry about my language, Cass. I didn't mean any disrespect."

Leroy shuffled his feet and twisted his hat. "The thing is, Doc. Me and Cass was thinking maybe we ought to call Opal, maybe have her go on out too. You know, maybe help with Clete and Karl."

Doc stared at Leroy. "Hell, why not? Maybe we ought to get the sheriff's wife out there too or the president of the Ladies Club. Jesus, Leroy."

Leroy didn't say a word.

"Oh hell, you're probably right. Call Opal. Jesus!" He opened the door and strode out.

Cass was already placing the call by the time Leroy closed the door behind him.

Mid-afternoon thunderheads were billowing high over the valley by the time Leroy and Doc Nelson began the half-mile hike along the river to the cabin. Lightning played along the tops of the hills, and the stagnant air seemed to vacuum the oxygen up into the pregnant clouds. Rain would have been a welcome relief. But no rain fell. Twice Leroy reached out to steady Doc as he stumbled along the path; both times he was rebuffed by an icy scowl as Doc jerked his arm away.

Clete was still sitting on the log staring into space as though he had lost the will to move or think. Doc did not even glance at him. He jerked open the door to the shack, staggering from the heat and smell before entering. He walked over to the bed.

"Karl, I need you to step outside so I can take care of Annie."

Karl tightened his grip on Annie's hand and did not move or look at the doctor.

Leroy stood in the doorway steeling himself, then followed Doc Nelson into the shack. Both men tried to reason with Karl, but the more they talked, the more Karl set his jaw. Doc's face was flushed and blotchy, his breathing ragged. Leroy felt ready to succumb to panic when the door flew open. Opal stood in the doorway, tiny and resolute, holding an armful of rags and a bucket of cleaning supplies.

She looked over the scene and appeared to size up the situation. Leroy expected her to melt down right there in the doorway, but instead she started barking orders like a drill sergeant.

"Leroy, you get Doc Nelson down to the creek and cool him off before he needs a doctor himself."

Doc started to object, but Opal talked right over him. "You can come back once you can take care of yourself. You ought to know better. If you have a heat stroke, how will that help anyone? Now go with Leroy before I have to haul you down there myself."

"Leroy, take this with you." She emptied the bucket and handed it to Leroy. Leroy took the bucket and led Doc by the elbow down to the river and into the shade of the willows. A few minutes later Opal came out and walked over to Clete. Leroy couldn't hear everything she said to him, but he sure heard what she said last.

"Clete, you're twenty-eight years old and it's high time you stopped thinking about yourself and started acting like a man. Now get up and get Karl out of there before we lose him too." She had Clete by both arms and was looking him square in the face when she said it. He didn't say a word, just got up and went inside the shack.

She came down to the river and loosened Doc's collar and commenced to lay into him about not taking care of himself at his age and with his heart. She dipped a rag in the stream to lay on his neck and badgered him into drinking more water. By the time Clete came out of the shack with Karl, Doc's color was returning to normal and he was back to his prickly self.

*****

(August 1971)

"She had me get Clete and Karl cooled off while she went back with the Doc. She come out twice to fill the bucket with water. I don't know how she stood it, being in there, but after the Doc examined Annie she sent him back down to set by the water again. He was grousing about it, but the heat had clean wiped him out. I had got Karl and Clete to take off their shoes and set down in the river and kept at them to drink more water like she had told me to do. I think all three of them might have had heat strokes if she hadn't come along. She cleaned Annie up and dressed her in a clean nightgown she found in that suitcase and stripped off all that bloody bedding and threw it right out the door. She was down on the floor scrubbing when I went back in.

"And then she commenced to working on Doc Nelson like she'd been working on that floor. I don't know if he would've gone along with it or not, but by the time he drove off with Annie's body he had agreed to put down the cause of death as pneumonia. Karl had wandered off down the river looking for those little boys and Opal ordered me to go round up a new mattress and bedding for him. She said she didn't care where I got it. It was dusk by the time I got back. I was just glad Betty was at her mother's. We had an old mattress and some blankets in a storage shed that I didn't think Betty would miss so I took those for Karl. When I got back Opal and Clete was waiting on the log and he was calm, – pale and sick looking, but calm. I helped her to fix up the bed, and Clete and me hauled that bloodied mattress and bedding out to my truck. I don't know what she told Harry about where she was – I guess that she was needed at Oleta's or some such story. I've been to war and I never seen anyone, man or woman, as tough as Opal was that day.

"The next day Clete picked up little Mae at Cass's and took her out to Oleta. And I guess you know the rest."

Leroy pulled a hankie from his back pocket and wiped his brow. "I could sure use a glass of water, if you don't mind." Leroy drained the glass in several gulps, then held it out for more. "Thank you, kindly, Jean."

Jean and Mae had interrupted Leroy frequently and pep-
pered him with questions, but for the hour or more that Leroy
had been speaking, Cloris had neither moved nor spoken.
Then, without saying a word to any of them, she shoved her
chair away from the table and strode out the back door and
off into the fields.

Jean half rose to follow her, but Leroy stopped her with a
hand laid gently on her arm.

"Let her be, Jean. Her and Clete are a lot alike. Most likely
she needs some thinking room."

Jean dropped back into her chair and silence as dead as
the air settled over them. Mae rummaged in her purse for a
bottle of aspirin and swallowed three.

"Mae, could you give me some of those too – and that bottle
opener?" Jean twisted around behind her to pull a coke from
the fridge. "Anyone else want a coke?"

"No thank you, Jean, none for me." Leroy shifted in his
chair and wiped his sweaty brow.

"I'll take one." Mae sat down and leaned toward Leroy.
Her pale blue eyes looked troubled and her voice trembled.

"Mr. Fulmer, do you think Mom knew the truth?"

Leroy worried his thumbnail and pondered Mae's question.
"Your mom's not a stupid woman. But she's always had this
way of seeing what she wanted to see. I suppose we all do that,
at least some of the time. But Oleta does it more than most
folks. As long as I've known her she's been flat-out crazy about
the movies, and what are movies but make-believe? Clete
didn't tell me what he told her, but she wanted that baby and
that must have been good enough for her. I doubt she asked
any questions she didn't want answers to. And your dad, well,
your dad and me never talked about it after that day. But he
was never the same. How could he have been? I don't think
I've ever seen him really happy again, not the way he used to
be. Seems like he tried to be a good husband to Oleta, at least
in those early years, and a good dad to you kids, but some-

thing was missing, like sometimes it is with a man after he comes back from a war. He must have seen Annie every time he looked at you, Mae. You look just like her. I don't know. Maybe Oleta and him should have gone their separate ways. Neither one of them ever seemed to know how to let up on the other."

Leroy stood and took his hat in his hands. "I don't think he ever could forgive himself and it destroyed him. Bitterness ain't no way to live. You've got to let it go when it comes a knocking. I know he wasn't always a perfect father, but he loved you girls. He just hated himself."

Leroy put on his hat and opened the screen door. "Give your mom my regards. I'll see that Steve takes good care of the place."

Chapter 19
Jean and Mae:
What the Heart Knows

(August, 1971)

The sun hung suspended low over the western horizon when Jean and Mae approached the cemetery late Saturday afternoon. Mae parked the car on the shoulder not far from Clete's grave.

"Look. Isn't that Mom?" Jean said.

On the opposite side of the cemetery near the old pioneer graves, Oleta was just getting into her car.

"I wonder why she parked clear over there?"

Mae and Jean followed her with their eyes as she turned the car around and drove away.

"I'm sort of glad we missed her. I want this time for the two of us, since you're leaving in the morning."

A light breeze caressed their cheeks as they walked downhill towards Clete's grave. The crisp smell of approaching autumn hung in the air. A few dry leaves, harbingers of fall, tumbled with the wind. The new sod atop Clete's grave had browned around the edges and the funeral flowers had withered and been removed, but lying on the grave was a fresh bouquet of Black-eyed Susans tied with a lavender ribbon. Jean laid the lavender dahlias they had brought with them from Cass's garden next to the yellow Black-eyed Susans.

"How about that. The colors match the ribbon on Mom's bouquet."

Arm-in-arm they stood quietly.

Mae broke the silence. "Why do you think Leroy told us about that day? I can't stop thinking about it. Do you think he's afraid we'll end up bitter like Dad?"

Jean looked down at Clete's fresh flower-bedecked grave. "Well, aren't we bitter? And Clark too? We've always taken Mom's side, even when she drove us nuts, but I don't know. Don't get me wrong. He did some unforgiveable things, but she wasn't blameless either. I just know I don't want to end up like him – or Cloris – pushing everyone away my whole life. I mean, look at us. All three of us do that."

Mae bent and traced Clete's name with her finger. "And I do it worst of all. Maybe that cycle needs to stop with us."

"I wonder where the twins are buried?"

"I have no idea, but it's not that big a cemetery. Let's look for them."

Jean and May went up and down the rows searching for the graves. Jean was sweeping debris away from the inscription on an old stone when Mae grabbed her arm and pointed at two graves tucked under a gnarly oak near the edge of the road. On each was a fresh bouquet of Black-eyed Susans tied with lavender ribbon.

Each grave had been cleaned and the area around them weeded. "I wonder how often Mom comes here?"

Jean shrugged her shoulders. "I wish she had brought us when we were kids. It feels like we're looking at the graves of strangers, and yet they were our brothers."

"Do you think Annie was buried here?" Mae asked.

"She must have been. Let's find her grave too."

In the fading light they walked up and down each row reading the stones, searching for the grave. They had all but given up when Jean suggested they go across the road to the old cemetery. Mae pulled open the rickety gate surrounding the small plot of land. On this side of the cemetery there was no lawn and no trees, just the same dried weeds and powdery dust as the surrounding hills. The graves here were mostly old, some dating back to pioneer days, and most of the stones were broken, dirt-encrusted and illegible. It took only a minute to spot a fresh grave on the north end. Karl's? Yes. And near it was a clean but weathered stone adorned with a cheerful bouquet of Black-eyed Susans, neatly tied with a lavender ribbon.

"She knows," Mae said. "She knows."

She knelt down and felt the lettering, reading the inscription out loud. "'Annie Adele Mueller, born January 19, 1921, died August 23, 1947.' My birthday."

"Kind of a rotten one this year," Jean said.

"No, not really. I learned who I am. And I learned who I don't want to be. It might be the best birthday gift I've ever been given." Mae stood. "How long do you think she's known?"

Jean hesitated. "I think she always knew."

Mae linked her arm with Jean's and they walked arm-in-arm between the graves and up the hill to the car. As they drove away a tumbleweed rolled down the hill in the stiffening breeze. In the twilight of evening a coyote howled.

* * * * *

(Two days later)

Jean parked the car on the side of the dusty road leading to the river. The dried grasses crunched underfoot and grasshoppers leaped ahead of her with each step. The shack looked just as forlorn as it had when she was there with Will, although it seemed months had passed since they had come that day on a whim.

She walked along the water's edge, then knelt down and found a flat rock to skim across the water. As she watched it bounce her thoughts skittered far away to another time. Turning, she made her way to the crumbling shack and pushed open the front door. She stood in the doorway taking it all in. Stepping carefully over the mounds of papers she placed a bouquet of Black-eyed Susans atop the pot-bellied stove and softly closed the door behind her. In the distance dust billowed behind a tractor. In the lifeless alkaline fields all was still.

CPSIA information can be obtained
at www.ICGtesting.com
Printed in the USA
FFHW02n0718210818
47764790-51459FF